Hardly Strangers

"This is the exact sort of romance novel I've been looking for: one that hinges on two adults who are messy and a little sloppy but evolving and trying to be better—but keyword: *adults*."

—Allison P. Davis, *New York* magazine writer and author of a forthcoming book about horniness

"Fresh, hot, and really f*cking fun. A vibrant portrait of what it's like to be young and pursuing a relationship in Los Angeles—or anywhere."

—Katrina Leno, author of *Everything All at Once* and *Summer of Salt*

"This book forced me to metabolize my own romantic edges and simultaneous hunger for love, allowing me to remember that perhaps this pursuit is one of the most human things we are known to want."

—Fariha Róisín, writer of *How to Cure a Ghost*, *Who Is Wellness For?*, and *Survival Takes a Wild Imagination*

Hardly Strangers

A.C. ROBINSON

831 STORIES

831 Stories

An imprint of Authors Equity
1123 Broadway, Suite 1008
New York, New York 10010

Cover design by C47.
Book design by Scribe Inc.
This is a work of fiction. Names, characters, places and incidents either
are products of the author's imagination or are used fictitiously.

Library of Congress Control Number: 2024943637
Print ISBN 9798893310207
Ebook ISBN 9798893310368

Printed in the United States of America

www.831stories.com
www.authorsequity.com

For Alexis,
let this serve as irrefutable proof
that your sage advice, tough love,
and faultless guidance are
never, ever wasted on me

Hardly
Strangers

I

Under different circumstances, maybe I'd be excited. Maybe I would be giving myself over to youthful optimism, listening to music, having a drink, and savoring the ritual of getting ready. Unfortunately, as it stands, I've surrendered to nerves and worry, staring at my own reflection in total silence like I'm preparing to deliver a dramatic Shakespearean monologue.

At this point, I hardly even see my face in the wooden vanity mirror—just bits and pieces. A pair of lips, almond-shaped eyes, a smattering of freckles against a warm background of brown skin—like an abstract painting. Shifting in my seat, I turn my attention to the jumbled assortment of pens, pots, and brushes strewn across the table. I'll obviously choose my go-to cat eye, a style that's evolved from the thick, clawlike blob my best friend Lexi once demonstrated on her own eyelids in our middle school bathroom to become the understated look I wear now. But still, presenting myself with the illusion of choice gives me something to do. A sense of control.

I pretend to consider my options as I twiddle absently with my necklace—a sterling silver hand with crossed fingers. The side of my thumb slides over the grooves and lines of the metal palm, following along to the twined fingertips as I let it fall against my chest, the reminder of its presence providing a small sense of comfort. It was a gift from my mother, one of many good luck charms and protective talismans she's given me over the years—my name, Shera, being another.

Shera—my mother's spelling-be-damned creative take on "Scheherazade," the narrator of *Arabian Nights*, who saves herself from execution at the hands of an embittered sultan by telling him elaborate, captivating folktales every night. She always said my name would weave some spell around me—that my words would carry me to safety, and as I told my stories, they would set me free.

True to my namesake, I am a storyteller—a writer, though a nonpracticing one at present. I haven't felt the spark of inspiration in ages, but I suppose I still find creative ways to tell "stories." This evening, for example, I'm using my gift to imagine every possible worst-case scenario for hours on end, envisioning each scene with vivid clarity like a screenplay, complete with dialogue and stage directions.

I guess I don't always know how to distinguish anxiety from intuition. These days, every turn of my stomach and throbbing heartbeat feels like a warning that my world is about to come crashing down, and—

No, tonight is different, I remind myself. Tonight, the uneasy feeling has a clear point of origin, an obvious explanation: in less than an hour, I'm finally going on a very-nearly-assured-but-not-quite-certain date with Michael.

I guess I have Lexi to thank for that too, for setting it all in motion when she urged—or rather, *forced*—me to accompany her to that folk music show four months ago . . .

It was October. My ability to stay home and wallow for days on end had reached Olympic-level dedication, so when Lexi called to invite me to what she described as a "Topanga Canyon thing" in the backyard of an antique shop, my practiced response of "Sorry, not tonight" was already in the chamber.

"Okay, I'm declaring martial law on this one," Lexi proclaimed over the phone. "I'm picking you up, and we're going—it's time to leave the cocoon."

After being unceremoniously hung up on, I stood frozen for a few minutes, debating whether or not defying my iron-willed childhood friend was even possible. In the end, I decided it was easier to accept my fate.

Topanga had been our longtime playground—a place we frequented as teens for its wild beauty and wilder parties. Now in our midtwenties, we rarely found ourselves trudging through overgrown fields in the pitch darkness to find hippie keggers, but the canyon still had an irresistible enchantment about it. That night was no different—chirping crickets intermingled with soft chatter as vintage-clad locals sprawled out over well-trod Persian rugs and slung themselves over battered velvet furniture. It had all been arranged in the middle of the yard beneath a rough-hewn wooden gazebo, resembling a makeshift outdoor living room. At the head, a man in a Canadian tuxedo perched on a rickety barstool playing Tim Buckley songs on an acoustic guitar, his eyes shut tight due to either overwhelming nervousness or overwhelming emotion. Listening intently and sipping

Two Buck Chuck from a paper cup as I sat huddled beside Lexi, I began to enjoy myself for the first time in what felt like eons.

A rugged, handsome stranger caught my eye almost immediately, standing a full head taller than most as he leaned cooly against one of the support posts, pushing his long, faintly unkempt California-brown hair behind his ear. I watched as he took a swig from a glass beer bottle, his lips enveloping its mouth, and felt a slight flutter in my stomach as his piercing gaze turned to me.

Meeting each other was a measured dance. Rising from my seat, I intentionally created a small disturbance, pushing gently through the throng of guests as I made my way to a seat on the store's craftsman porch steps just behind the crowd and lit an American Spirit. I hoped he would join me—I didn't really smoke, but I'd learned to use cigarettes as props for the purpose of getting both in and out of social situations. Though the stranger stole a casual glance back, observing my display with what looked like a small, knowing smile, he still made me wait a good ten minutes and two cigarettes before making his way over.

"Mind if I get one of those?"

I turned as he announced his presence, propping one of his sturdy made-in-America Frye boots up on the step beside me and settling into another casual lean against the railing. He looked good leaning, though it crossed my mind that he seemed a little posed.

"Sure." I handed him a cigarette with a flicker of satisfaction, studying his face as I did so. Midthirties, world worn, sunbaked skin. Probably an occasional surfer, but more of a cowboy than a beach bum.

"I'm Michael, by the way."

"Shera."

"*Sher-uh*," he repeated. "That's an interesting name—never heard it before. What does it mean?"

I considered just how much of a history lesson Michael really wanted, but before I could answer, he leaned forward, squinting slightly as he stared intently into my face.

"Wait—what color are your eyes?"

"Hazel. Or green sometimes—but mostly hazel."

I fumbled for the words slightly, my heartbeat quickening under the heat of his gaze as I realized it was the first contact I'd had with someone I found attractive in a long while. Suddenly the "cigarette break" move felt too daring—like I practically asked him to fuck me right then and there with my subtle beckoning. Now that he had come, I didn't quite know what to do with him.

"That's wild," Michael said, running a hand over his stubbly chin. "So where are you from—*originally*?"

It was a question I'd become somewhat accustomed to from an early age. Growing up in a still pre–racially conscious Los Angeles with olive-brown skin, dark 4A hair perpetually worn in braids, and light eyes—the collaborative product of my Black mother and fair-skinned Louisiana Creole father—meant that it was most often posed by middle-aged, surgically taut Caucasian women in its more jarring form: "What *are* you?" I wasn't bothered by curiosity, just the framing that made me feel divorced from humanity in some small way.

I told Michael I grew up around Venice Beach, in an apartment off Ocean Park, but from his continued curious expression, I could tell that wasn't the answer he was looking for. Regardless, I asked him the same, and he said he was a transplant from

Seattle, having only recently settled after finding the perfect yurt/ guesthouse to live in.

"Well, since you're new to LA, I'd like to offer my services as an official tour guide," I said, daring myself to flirt more openly. "I live in Silver Lake, which is basically on the other side of the world, but maybe I can show you around my neighborhood sometime."

Michael smiled, but before he had a chance to respond, Lexi bounded up beside us, her sandy-blonde hair frizzy in the night air as she buried her nose in the fluffy collar of her vintage Penny Lane coat.

"I gotta get out of here, Sher. Too cold."

I felt my heart sink, disappointment flooding through me at the thought of what could have progressed with a little more time, but I only nodded, rising and turning to Michael.

"Well—guess I'm off."

"It was nice to meet you, *Sher-uh*." He exaggerated the pronunciation again—a callback I suppose I was meant to find endearing but was slightly irked by instead.

Without warning, Michael stepped forward and pulled me into a warm embrace, my nose pressed against his chest. His large hands moved over my back, one resting in the curve of my spine and the other crawling upward, holding me steady between the shoulder blades. His size, his warmth, his body, I couldn't remember the last time I'd—

"I'll see ya around," he said, breaking away suddenly and halting my train of thought. It took me a moment to collect myself—I hardly remembered walking to the car.

On the drive home, I asked Lexi about Michael, and she

informed me that though she hadn't personally met him before that evening, she'd heard about him.

"He's a filmmaker, or wannabe at least. He hasn't been here long, but everyone's calling him the 'Babe of the Canyon.'" She passed a hand in an arc through the air as she announced his title like she was painting the words in lights. "You know, it's kinda like a small town up there—he's fresh meat, and the ladies want a piece."

"*Fuck.*"

"Sher, c'mon. I can feel you caving in," she said, astutely predicting the trajectory of my runaway thoughts. "Sometimes, that's just how it goes when someone's hot—there's a little healthy competition. You know, it's like you automatically assume someone else will be chosen over you . . ." She trailed off as a dark, murky silence filled the car.

"I know." I placed a reassuring hand on her shoulder. "I'm working on it."

Lexi was integral to my survival that terrible year. She was a good friend, and I didn't want her to fear stepping on one of my trip wires . . .

My own eyes in the mirror bring me back to the present moment—to my studio apartment and the slight February chill creeping in despite the valiant efforts of my ancient wall heater. That and the sound of footsteps approaching along the corridor outside, stopping just before my apartment. No knock or hello. In typical Lexi fashion, the door swings open, and she steps inside.

"Oh my god—Sher. Did you kill someone? It smells *overwhelmingly* of bleach in here."

She pulls off her bright-orange peacoat and throws it on a

waiting armchair before walking past me to my designated "bed-room corner." After unzipping her too-tight, sky-high-waisted vintage Wranglers, she falls back onto the bed with a tired huff.

"Okay, so tell me what he said again *exactly*."

"I don't . . . even . . . remember . . ." I reply, my words punctu-ated by concentrated strokes as I draw on the signature eyeliner. I turn to look at Lexi.

"Whatever it was, it was just kind of . . . vague."

The initial doubt crept in sometime around noon as I sat on the couch with my too-strong cup of espresso, obsessively going over the night before—when I entered the kitchen of a house party in Echo Park to find Michael rooting around in the fridge . . .

We said hello and made small talk for a while, comparing and contrasting our mental Rolodexes of mutual friends in atten-dance and revealing how we knew them. I watched his face as I spoke—his eyes flickering down to my mouth and back to meet my own, again and again. In four months of run-ins around town, he always remained interminably seductive, never miss-ing an opportunity to grab my hand to examine some piece of jewelry or wink at me from across the room—but nothing had evolved beyond that.

Maybe it was the two glasses of earthy, pungent orange wine I had over the evening, or maybe I felt emboldened by the fact that he was on my side of town for a change, but suddenly, I found myself taking action.

"What are you doing tomorrow night?" I blurted.

Michael considered for a moment, squinting up as if his social calendar was written on the ceiling. "Not sure—why?"

"Do you want to grab a drink at Bar Sperl in Silver Lake around nine?"

Michael's affirmative, albeit slightly ambiguous, response had become warped and blurry in my anxious recollection. Something in the ballpark of "I'll probably be in the area—yeah. Maybe I'll swing by."

I replayed the scene in my head all afternoon, trying to draw clear confirmation from the simple interaction like water from a stone. What began as a banal reassessment spiraled into all-out mental warfare as I played and replayed cinematic visions of myself sitting at the bar alone, glancing eagerly toward the door with every new entry before realizing I was entirely mistaken.

I spent the rest of the day attempting to quell my nerves as I always did: with meditative housework. What began with some basic tidying devolved into a frenzied obsession as I tried to bleach my dingy bathtub back to its former glory until the fumes made my head spin . . .

"God, that's so fucking *typical*." Lexi rolls onto her side to face me. "Men are so commitment-phobic, they can't even commit to plans on a Saturday night."

I chuckle despite the acid reflux that's been burning like bubbling magma in my chest for hours. Lexi raises her eyebrows slightly, assuming the look she always does when she's about to bully me into a sense of confidence.

"Don't worry. Warren and I will be there the whole time as backup. We'll have some drinks, some laughs, and if Canyon Babe doesn't show up, it'll be his loss. His. Fucking. Loss!" She pounds her fist against the duvet to emphasize each of these last words.

The plan Lexi concocted a few hours prior: She and our friend

Warren would accompany me to Bar Sperl like any other night. If Michael showed up, they would make themselves scarce, and I'd enjoy my date. If he didn't, they would each buy me a shot, and we would go to some celebutante's party in the Hollywood Hills.

"Bottom line, regardless of what happens, I feel like this is an important step," Lexi continues. "You're announcing to the universe that you're ready for something new . . ." She slows, measuring her next words carefully. "That your heart is still open."

"Thanks, Lex." I smile tightly. I'm lucky to have her near-constant cheerleading, but today, it feels like tonguing a canker sore. Returning to the same wounded point again and again, unable to move in the right direction without some reminder of the wrong from whence I came.

I decide I'm content with my makeup, ending with a swipe of my favorite drugstore lipstick—a rosy-brown color that Lexi first shoplifted for me when we were fifteen. At long last, I stand.

"Do I look okay?"

She eyes my outfit. I chose a form-fitting, slightly sheer black turtleneck that's long enough to cover my midriff but short enough to leave a ribbon of flesh visible above my loose black slacks. Hints of silver break up the darkness, gleaming from the buckle of a thick leather belt, the assortment of large sterling rings Lexi found for me over the years, and, of course, my lucky hand necklace. I finish it off with my prized possession—an elegant wool Prada blazer I thrifted by chance years ago in the Valley. Lexi hates that I almost exclusively wear black—as the owner of an online vintage shop, she's pushed the crème de la crème of stunning, colorful clothing on me for years to absolutely no avail.

Still, I see a flicker of pride in her eyes every time I wear the rings she hand-selected.

"*Ah*, a change of pace! If I'm not mistaken, you've gone for more of an *onyx* black here instead of your typical *pitch* black, yes?"

I glare at Lexi until she concedes. "Fine." She rolls her eyes as her face spreads into a small smile. "You look gorg—great jewelry."

She struggles momentarily to rise from the bed, constricted by the tightness of her jeans, but after some effort, she stands, zipping them with a sharp intake of breath as she turns to face me.

"Okay, so, *remember* . . ." She points a finger, her eyes locked intently on mine. "No matter what happens, tonight is a new beginning." I give a shallow nod, but her index is joined by her raised thumb to form a finger gun as she barks, "*Say* it! I want to hear it."

My face cracks into a smile as I repeat, "Tonight is a new beginning."

"Good." Lexi's furrowed brow softens as she lowers her weapon with a broad grin. "Alright. Let's do this."

I watch my friend, a flicker of something foreign igniting within me. A feeling I rarely allow myself to have for fear that if it flies me to the highest heights, it can just as easily send me plummeting back to earth. It's hope—the thing with feathers. For just a moment, I feel cleansed of the past year—an empty page, ready to be blackened with the ink of a different story. Assured by a knowledge from somewhere deep within that tonight will indeed be the start of something new.

II

It's 9:02 p.m. when we arrive at Bar Sperl, a moody, dimly lit place on Sunset Boulevard modeled after a classic French brasserie, with parquet wood floors, tufted leather booths, and ornate ceiling molding. It's rumored that the owner, a temperamental, once-successful contemporary artist from Vienna, changes his mind about permitting smoking on the small back patio depending on whether or not he has personally decided to quit that particular week. It's one of those places that has seen many a renaissance over the years, waxing and waning with cool factor time and time again, but to us, regardless of popularity, it's always held some adolescent magic—a glamour that calls out every weekend with the promise of possibility.

I compulsively pull my phone out of my leather shoulder bag for the ten thousandth time as Lexi and I prepare to show our IDs to the surly, muscled bouncer seated outside. Quietly returning to my text log with Michael, I swallow hard as I see that my own message from hours earlier—a panicked confirmation of the timeliness with which I would be arriving—is still unanswered.

I can feel the tendrils of doubt like climbing ivy, slithering through the cracks in those mental walls I only just erected and fortified. Maybe I've been misreading Michael—maybe I've mistaken kindness for flirting, and his noncommittal response was a casual attempt to let me down easy.

I quickly scan my memory bank of our prior interactions, one run-in a few weeks back standing out . . .

I'd been assisting Lexi most Sundays at an art, wine, and vintage pop-up at a gallery in Venice where we spent most of our time perusing the other vendors' stalls in shifts. When Michael appeared out of nowhere at our booth, Lexi all but forced me to "take a break."

He and I spent a little while exploring the space, assessing the various paintings and sculptures on display and eventually discussing his own art—a short film he was making about a woman who talks to God through a practice of compulsive masturbation.

"Sorry, I know the subject matter can be a little . . . awkward for some people," he said, furrowing his brow with a look of something like pity.

"No, not at all. I love the concept!" I responded a bit more emphatically than I intended. In truth, I found the whole thing a little tired, but I hated the idea of him seeing me as prudish.

"Yeah? You just looked a little tense for a minute there." He laughed, his tone vaguely patronizing. "Here, let me give you a quick shoulder rub."

The sudden offer surprised me—I stared wide-eyed for a moment, waiting for him to tell me he was kidding.

"C'mere." He beckoned with a small tilt of his head. "I've been told I have magic hands. May I?"

I made some nervous chirping sound in the affirmative as I turned my back, and he stepped behind me, peeling my jacket down from my shoulders to reveal the black silk slip dress beneath it. I felt my face flush as his warm hands slid over my bare shoulders, his thumbs slowly, expertly working into my muscles, pushing and pulling me closer to his body.

"Inhale," he commanded, his voice a low growl in my ear as I obeyed. "And exhale." I breathed out, softening into his firm grasp. When he withdrew his touch, a faint, involuntary moan escaped my lips that I hoped he didn't hear but feared he did.

That somewhat charged moment concluded with Michael telling me I was "really tight" and "should probably look into having some consistent bodywork done." That was when he asked for my phone number to send me the contact for his deep-tissue acupuncturist—a Dr. Marnie Lightfoot, who worked out of her meditation room in Reseda. At the time, I assumed it was a ploy, but after I texted a warm thank-you for Dr. Lightfoot's information, the conversation petered out immediately . . .

"*Sher.*" Lexi's snapping fingers disrupt the warm, fluttery, and confusing memory as I look up to see the bouncer waiting impatiently for me.

"Sorry," I mumble, shoving the phone back into my bag and handing over my driver's license. He scrutinizes it for a moment longer than necessary, quite possibly as retribution for my inattention, before handing it back.

Following Lexi inside, I clock only a small handful of patrons seated around the bar, our third musketeer, Warren, being one of them. He waves when he sees us, his chest-length brown hair bobbing gently around his freckled face.

"Bathroom," Lexi announces in place of a greeting when we reach our companion. "Get me a whiskey ginger?"

"Hi to you too, Lex," Warren says as she beelines for the back. I give him a small half hug before taking a seat beside him.

We wordlessly eye the two bartenders—one a tall, pale ginger-haired man with a flashy smile, and the other a slender, dark-skinned woman with a slicked-back bun standing stone-faced as she rattles a cocktail shaker. As regulars, we know them both—the redhead is Daryl, a wannabe actor who frequently gives Lexi free drinks, and the girl is Nicole, Warren's current crush to whom he has never managed to say more than a few words.

"Tonight's the night." I pat Warren on the shoulder teasingly, and he swallows hard, smiling at Nicole as she stares straight ahead.

"I'm gonna talk to her."

He sounds confident—as if he hasn't been promising to do so for months. We only learned her name a few weeks back, and Lexi was the one to ask.

Warren leans over, raising a timid hand as he attempts to position himself in his crush's eyeline, but before he can reach her, Daryl intercepts.

"Hey, guys, what can I get for you?" He grins, revealing his perfect toothpaste-commercial teeth.

"Hi," I interject as Warren stares mutely. "One whiskey ginger, a vodka soda for me, and—" I turn to my spellbound companion. He's caught Nicole's eye, and she's now glaring back suspiciously.

"Uh, tequila soda."

Daryl smirks as he busies himself with our order, finishing just as Lexi appears, taking a seat on the other side of Warren.

"Weak, per usual." She grimaces with her first sip. "Daryl! Can I get a round of shots too?"

She shrugs off her coat, revealing the strappy, thin white camisole she's wearing without a bra. Daryl surveys Lexi, his eyes darting down to her chest as he flashes his winning smile again and pours three heavy-handed shots of our respective liquors.

"To endless possibilities. On the count of three—you too, Daryl!" Lexi commands as she lifts her vial and waits for the bartender to pour his own.

"One, two—" We down them on three. My mouth begins watering with that rainy, sick feeling immediately, but I hold it down, coughing slightly as the burn of my anxious brooding from earlier meets the burn of well vodka.

"There—the night begins," Lexi announces triumphantly, slamming her glass on the bar and grinning at the pair of us as we both recover.

"*Look!*" she exclaims, grabbing Warren's arm before proceeding in a stage whisper. "Nicole's here!" Both bartenders look up as Warren's pale face becomes flushed with rosy color.

Lexi has always had a volume-control issue—she shouts everything, and there's nothing to be done about it. I learned years ago that asking her to lower her voice does nothing but cause her to sour and give me the silent treatment as a demonstration of just how quiet she can be.

"Thank you for that." He chuckles ruefully, rubbing at his forehead as Lexi gapes with incredulity.

"What? No one can hear me!" I try to stifle my snicker as she glares at the two of us.

"Okay, fuck both of you. So *what* if she hears? You like her, right?" Warren's hand remains glued to his face, shielding his eyes as Lexi pulls at his wrists.

I watch the pair of them for a moment, two peas in a pod—the very picture of California natives with their sun-licked hair and sea-brined skin. I always secretly thought they looked good together and told Lexi so, but after they shared a drunken make-out a few years back, one that seemed to traumatize them both in equal measure, the notion was forever put to bed. "Like kissing a *cousin*," Lexi recounted the next day over the phone as my shoulders shook with laughter. Later, I heard a similar review from Warren, though he said it felt like kissing his mother.

"You like her, you *do*." Lexi's tone turns parental, and I smirk as she continues to lecture Warren. "But you're so afraid of rejection that you never take a chance. Look at Shera." She pauses, shifting her heat-seeking gaze over to me. "Shera wouldn't be going on a date if she hadn't decided to be bold. She'd probably be at home in bed right now, smelling the clothes she was wearing last night and hoping, *praying* she could still get a whiff of him on them—" Lexi stops, raising a defensive hand as I dip my fingers in my drink and flick the droplets at her.

"*Enough*, girls," Warren says, playing along with a tone of mock authority. "Yes, *very* brave, and I'm a coward—but to be fair, Shera doesn't even know if she *is* going on a date."

Lexi glowers at him, a hint of concern on her face as she turns her attention to me. I can read her so easily after all these years—the pleading in the slight upturn of her lips, her eyes begging for me to stay afloat. It's tiring being treated like I'm made of glass, but I know that she only does so because she watched me shatter into a million pieces. I will myself to quiet the pang of anxiety Warren's words generate and force a smile.

"It's true—I'm only about forty percent sure I have a date

tonight," I begin slowly. "But that's still a one hundred percent better chance of getting laid than you have."

Warren purses his lips, nodding slowly in acceptance as Lexi crows gleefully, relieved to see me resist deflation.

"So if all goes well tonight—does that mean you're gonna . . ." She trails off, dramatically raising and lowering her eyebrows like a cartoon character. I open my mouth to reply, but Warren suddenly interrupts.

"Wait, guys—don't look now, but Shera has an admirer."

"Where?" Lexi glances around wildly despite his instructions, but I remain steady. I have been feeling it for some time now—the distinctive psychic itch that occurs when a pair of eyes are fixed on you.

"On the end over there, the one in black. It's Max King."

"Who?" Lexi and I say in unison. She's now staring over my shoulder, evaluating, but I still haven't turned. I try to glean what the man looks like from the expression on her face, but she's oddly unreadable.

"He's the lead singer of this punk band, Dog from Hell—"

"Stupid name," Lexi interjects. Warren sighs, exasperated.

"Lyrically, their songs are actually really poetic, and Max has this kind of spoken-word style of singing, but then the music itself is rhythmically heavy with, like, super gritty guitar and—" Warren stops, glancing side to side as he realizes that both Lexi and I are not paying close enough attention to his analysis. "Anyway, I'm actually kind of a fan." He shifts in his seat, turning squarely to face me with a preparatory look on his face like he's about to suggest we go in on a timeshare together. "You should go talk to him."

I shake my head dismissively in answer, but while their faces are fixed on mine, it's the perfect time to steal a glance. I turn slowly, looking up as if I'm searching for one label in particular within the rows and rows of shelved liquor bottles. As I lower my eyes to the patrons staggered around the curved, L-shaped bar, one man sitting at the far end meets my gaze.

Beneath a shaggy mod-like haircut, his thickly knitted brows catch my attention first—slanted in severe, angled lines above unflinching brown eyes. His chiseled jaw and strong, faintly aquiline nose somehow accentuate the cupid's bow of his upper lip, thin in comparison to the fullness of his lower. He's a little pale but handsome, I suppose—though there's something in his unwavering stare that unnerves me. I hold it for a moment longer, deciding for some reason that I don't like the idea of him winning—like a game of chicken. As if he can hear my thoughts, his lips spread into a small, devilish smile.

"I'm not going over there," I snort, snapping my attention back to Warren. "If you're a fan, *you* should go talk to him."

I can practically feel my phone burning a hole in my purse, calling out to me. I rummage around for it, my heart sinking slightly as I withdraw it to find that I have no new messages. The large white numerals read 9:31 p.m. I assumed that if Michael was coming, he wouldn't be on time, but I wonder just how long I'll have to wait before his decision becomes clear.

"He's cute." Lexi continues to squint at the man across the bar. "But the staring is freaky—Sher, stop worrying, I can feel you. Michael will be here any minute—I have a sixth sense about it, I'm telling you." She pauses, studying my still-downturned face before pivoting to Warren with a mixture of pleading and menacing. "C'mon, give Shera a pep talk from the male perspective."

"My male perspective is that Michael sounds like a *douchebag*—" Warren begins, but Lexi cuts him off with a hard poke in the ribs. "Sorry." He grunts, recovering from the attack. "But really, if he doesn't show up, then he's an idiot."

Lexi and I both watch him, waiting for more pearls of wisdom, but he only shrugs silently.

"Yes—exactly," Lexi says, casting a withering look toward Warren. She opens her mouth to deliver what will undoubtedly be an epic sermon of self-empowerment, but before she can continue, a familiar face appears beside her.

"Oh, *hello*!"

My stomach lurches at the sound of Emily's voice. She's a good friend of Lexi's, though decidedly not one of mine. Lexi stands, squealing excitedly as Emily embraces her in a long hug, and Warren glances at me with a smirk. We've spoken about our mutual distaste in private—Emily astutely recognized Lexi's value as a truly one-of-a-kind friend when they met a few years back, and while she puts a tremendous amount of care and concern into their budding relationship, she also puts a considerable amount of effort into competing with me for Lexi's undivided attention. It began subtly—plans and weekend getaways from which I was always conveniently excluded. But with Lexi's most ardent tending to me over the last year, Emily's thinly veiled jealousy of our unbreakable bond has become far more apparent. I try to see her distaste for what it is, but I mostly fail.

"What are you up to tonight?" Emily asks, still refusing to acknowledge Warren and me. I pray that Lexi will have the good sense not to tell her.

"Shera has a date!" Lexi replies, gesturing toward me as I sheepishly put up a hand in greeting.

Emily flicks a lock of dyed-blonde hair behind her shoulder, her ice-blue eyes twinkling with intrigue. I wonder for a moment if the recent change in hair color has something to do with Lexi—Warren has long joked that Emily has an air of "*Single White Female*-ness" about her.

"A *date*," Emily croons. "Exciting—is he here?"

"Not yet." Lexi jumps in defensively, a flicker of realization at her potential mistake apparent in her tone. Emily smiles like a crocodile, nodding slowly.

"Oh, well, I'm glad you're getting back out there—after everything."

I smile back despite the fire smoldering in my stomach. She knows the whole story, of course. By now, it's common gossip, but something in that smile—

"I'll be back."

I rise without another word, the fire suddenly replaced by an unexpected watery welling of emotion. I think of my carefully drawn makeup and grit my teeth, willing myself not to ruin my hard work as I head for the bathroom. Though I've hardly touched my drink, the shot from earlier has filled me with a subtle warmth that I can feel now as I move.

This, my sensitivity—this is why Lexi keeps me sheathed in bubble wrap. I can't be irritated with anyone for treading lightly when I'm still clearly made of eggshells. I watch the water from the sink run over my sterling rings for a few minutes, like a cold rushing stream over time-worn stones. Looking up to meet my reflection, I study myself in the narrow mirror, realizing I don't look the way I feel. The oddly flattering bathroom light has turned my eyes to pure amber, set into my angular face and framed elegantly by my long braids. I look steady and enigmatic, sexy even—all wrapped in black. I look like the kind of woman who can hold her own, someone who wouldn't be phased by an offhand comment, and yet—here I am, hiding in the bathroom. That reflection is a stranger, a costume worn by a fraud.

No, I think to myself, *no more self-pity, no more wallowing. Tonight is different—a new chapter. A different story.*

I reapply my lipstick and stand there for a moment longer, taking several deep, steadying breaths before gathering myself to go back to the bar.

I return to find that during my brief departure, Bar Sperl has filled to the brim. Remembering why I'm here, I begin to move more slowly, surveilling the crowd in search of Michael's towering figure. Suddenly, the psychic itch returns—the feeling that I'm being watched by someone just behind me. His warmth and scent greet me before his words.

"Hello."

The sound is soft and close, issuing from lips that are mere inches from my ear. I turn to find myself face-to-face with Max King.

III

"Hi," I reply, my tone vaguely suspicious.

"How's it going?" The fullness of his lilting Irish accent becomes apparent as his mouth encircles each vowel. He's only a couple of inches taller than me, I guess five foot ten, maybe eleven, but there's a commanding air about him that feels slightly intimidating.

"It's going," I say flatly.

"What were you celebrating?"

"What?"

"Your friend there was making a toast. What were you celebrating?" He gestures with his nose toward the bar, his hands firmly buried in the pockets of his black leather jacket.

I stare for a moment, the gears of my mind whirring slowly, catching on to Emily's reptilian smile, Michael's absence, and Warren's brief introduction of the man who stands before me, blocking the way back to my seat.

"Oh, nothing. I—I have a date."

"A *date*!" His look is one of amusement. It reminds me of Emily's reaction to the same news, and I feel my face prickle with heat. I can't fathom why I've even told him.

"Yes, a fucking date. Do you have a problem with that?" I snap, surprising even myself. Something about him, his audacity and unwavering sureness, has dissolved my standard practice of social niceties.

"I suppose not." He shrugs, glancing around the room. "Just wondering when this mystery man of yours will appear. You have been here a while now."

I look back to where Lexi and Warren are still seated. They're alone again, thankfully, and regarding my interaction with wide, inquisitive eyes—though they aren't the only ones. I notice the handful of strangers watching us—or watching *him*, rather—their faces bright with varying degrees of awareness, from casual recognition to unapologetic admiration. I'm sure he's accustomed to the attention, practiced in the act of pretending as if he can't feel it on him—as if he can't hear the whispers.

"How do you know the guy I'm with isn't him?" I ask defiantly.

"What, the one who's been staring at that lovely bartender all night?"

I glare at him silently. He looks like a wolf standing there, eyeing me with hunger wet and glistening in the small parting of his lips, and yet—there's something almost familiar about him. His eyes search my face, and I see a genuine desire for the truth.

"My date isn't here yet. In fact, I don't even know if it is a date, but here I am—waiting, I guess." I sigh heavily, hoisting my purse back over my shoulder from where it's slipped.

"Well, he's a fool then." He furrows his brow and leans in as if he's about to share a secret, the sweet scent of his cologne filling my nostrils. "Look at you—any man would be lucky to have you."

I feel myself melting under his gaze, like standing under the narrowed light beam of a magnifying glass. For the first time, I note the small, dark beauty mark sitting above the left side of his upper lip, bringing an almost feminine quality to the defined curve of his mouth. He shifts suddenly from seductive intensity back into that devilish grin.

"I'm Max."

"Shera."

"Lovely to meet you, Shera." He inclines his head slightly with an air of play propriety. I like the way my name sounds coming from his mouth, and I begrudgingly allow a small smile to come to my lips. I move to turn away from him, but he quickly sidesteps, obstructing my path once more.

"Come for a walk with me."

"Absolutely not," I snort incredulously. "I'm going back to my friends—please move."

Max puts up his hands defensively as if to show that he won't try to physically stop me. "Look, just a quick one to the gas station up the road there for a pack of cigs." He takes a small step closer, and I can feel the heat of him. "Come with me."

I stare at him, and he meets my gaze with equal force. Unlike Michael's passive nonattachment, Max's desire is unambiguous, clear as day in the unflinching focus with which his eyes rove my lips and run the length of my body. No self-consciousness, no hesitation—as if his need outweighs all reason, all judgment, all possibility of humiliating rejection. I feel my pulse quicken, the drumming of my heartbeat rivaling the barroom din as I try to hold firm against the hunger in his eyes—the hunger that I fear may be finding its mirror in my own.

I should return to my friends, to the safety of waiting, waiting, waiting—but instead, as if in a trance, I hear the words roll off my tongue before I have even the faintest chance of stopping them: "Okay—but it has to be quick."

He grins victoriously. "We'll be back in a flash."

I lead the charge toward the front door, holding Lexi's perplexed gaze as I weave through the crowded room, my suitor in tow. As we approach my friends, the looks on their faces make it clear that I owe some explanation.

"Um, I'm—we're going to get cigarettes," I say, pausing momentarily beside the pair of them as they stare like screech owls. Max stops just behind me, the hawklike look on his face replaced by a pleasant warmth as he smiles at Warren and Lexi.

"I'm Max, and I swear I'm not a serial killer."

Lexi chuckles awkwardly as she tries to communicate with me through eye contact. "What are you *doing?*" I interpret her words telepathically as her face remains fixed with a puzzled expression. Even if she said it aloud, I wouldn't have the faintest idea how to answer.

"I'll be right back," I assure my friends, the words serving as a reminder for Max as well.

The brisk night air feels soothing as we step out onto the street and set off on our walk toward the Chevron sign glowing in the near distance.

"So," Max begins, "what's the story with this date of yours?"

"There isn't much to tell," I reply, still perplexed by my own willingness to be open with him. "I've known the guy for a little while now, I guess, and last night, I asked if he wanted to meet me here."

"And he said?"

"Something like . . . 'Maybe I can swing by.'"

"But he hasn't."

"No." I sigh, exhausted by what feels like an endless repetition of those words.

He allows the information to hang in the air between us for a moment before replying, "Seems like a sound guy." I roll my eyes at him in answer.

"So what makes this one good enough to wait for?" he continues as we stop at a crosswalk. "Have you fucked him?" The question comes with the same genuine, casual curiosity as the rest of his questions.

"No," I reply slowly, suppressing a reaction that will surely only cause him to dig in deeper. His barrage of queries is beginning to feel like the shameless, endless probing of a precocious child.

"What are you into then?"

"Into?" The glowing white walk signal urges us across the street as he stares straight ahead.

"In the bedroom, I mean."

The drumbeat of my heart quickens, heat rising in my ears. I wonder if it's an intimidation tactic, a forward attempt to make me squirm, but as we reach the gas station and our faces become bathed in cold fluorescent light, I turn to see that same look of unfeigned intrigue on his face.

"And why on earth would I tell a complete stranger something like that?"

"A *stranger*? That hurts, Shera." Max stops and claps a hand over his heart dramatically. I roll my eyes again, my mouth twitching as I suppress a smile. "Well, that may be at the moment," he continues, taking a step forward to close the gap between us as he leans in just inches from my face. "But I've got this funny feeling we won't be strangers for long."

I open my mouth in protest, but he winks with a cheeky smirk and walks backward toward the convenience store, his mirthful eyes fixed on me.

It feels like the intermission of a play as I stand outside, watching Max through the glass windows. Waiting here on the sidewalk, the reality of the situation is difficult to ignore, especially since any effects from the very small amount of alcohol I imbibed earlier have worn off completely now. I have no excuse for following that magnetic pull I feel toward him.

I withdraw my phone for the first time since I checked back at the bar—9:58 p.m., nearly an hour since we arrived. I have two texts from Lexi, one from when I ran off to the restroom and the other sent just after I left with Max.

Are you okay? Do you need me?

I'm so confused. What is going on???

I look up to see Max emerging from the store, tapping a pack of cigarettes with his palm as he walks toward me. I quickly type out a reply.

Honestly, I have no idea. Is Michael there?

Her response is almost immediate.

No Michael but Warren finally spoke to Nicole.

And??

He said "Your hair is really . . . smooth"

Ah. Better luck next time.

No Michael. I drop my phone back into the black abyss of my purse—no need for it anymore. No need for checking and wondering and worrying now—I've been stood up. In all likelihood, at this very moment, Michael's leaning against the smooth dark wood of some other bar with some other girl, detailing what he envisions for the final act of his short film when his female protagonist orgasms so intensely that she dies.

I hardly notice Max standing in front of me, offering the pack of Marlboros in his outstretched hand. I shake my head—the roiling in my belly has returned, and I'm not in the mood for a cigarette, but I watch while he lights his, the butt of it resting softly between his lips as the warm firelight chisels his face with shadow. We walk the first block in an oddly comfortable silence, Max smoking as I remain lost in thought.

"What's your man's name then?" he asks, flicking his cigarette as we cross the street. He withdraws a packet of gum from his pocket and offers me a stick.

"Thanks," I reply, grateful for the act of chewing as a means of steadying my nerves. I consider the harm in telling him before replying.

"His name's Michael."

"Michael," Max repeats, chewing thoughtfully as he considers his next question. "And what does he look like?"

I pull a fantasy image—Michael standing shirtless at the foot of my bed, his fingers slowly undoing the button of his jeans as he smiles down at me, a stray lock of hair dangling over one eye.

I shrug dismissively. "Tall, tan, blue eyes."

"*Pretty boy*," Max says teasingly. "Is that your type?"

The faces of my past lovers, both real and imagined, flash through my mind—a diverse cast of characters with no two bearing any real resemblance.

"I don't have a type."

Max nods but says nothing. I steal glances at the side of his face curiously as we chew and walk in silence. He seems to be deep in thought, his brow furrowed in what appears to be a look of quiet deliberation—or perhaps nervousness. It's a look I haven't seen yet, a departure from the unwavering sureness he's exhibited since that first moment our eyes met across the bar.

"Your eyes are beautiful, by the way," he says suddenly.

"Thank you."

"They remind me of this short story, 'Dark They Were, and Golden-Eyed.' It's—"

"I know it," I interrupt enthusiastically, forgetting myself for a moment. "By Ray Bradbury. About the Bittering family escaping war on Earth by building a colony on Mars—it's one of my favorites."

Max smiles at my exuberance. "Yeah, me too. I always imagined the Martians to look a bit like, well—like you."

"Should I be offended?"

"Not at all—I mean it as a compliment. You have an otherworldliness about you." He spits his gum into a trash can as we pass.

"It's more than the look of you. It's something else I can't quite put into words."

I swallow hard, searching for an adequate response to his apparent sincerity, but as we reach the mouth of the alleyway that runs between a small collection of shops and Bar Sperl, Max grabs my hand, pulling me gently into the shadows. His touch is warm and firm—I'm struck by the immediate comfort of it as I realize this is the first time we've made any physical contact. No hug or handshake in greeting, no nudge or brush against each other until now.

"What are you doing?"

"Can I kiss you?"

"What?"

There's no bite in my tone now—any fire I may have meant to wield against him has become a steady, simmering warmth, rising from somewhere deep within and spreading throughout my entire body. Our fingers remain entwined as he pulls me closer.

"Can I kiss you?" he repeats, lower, quieter than before.

I feel the cogs of my mind whirring, trying to make sense, desperate for order, for rationality and reason—but there is none. There's only Max's dark eyes and parted lips, his scent, and the warmth of his body, mere inches from mine.

"Yes—you can."

He smiles as he takes my face in his hands, the feel of his fingers sending rolling waves up and down my spine. I brace for impact, but it doesn't come straightaway—instead, he remains still for a moment, studying every inch, every feature until heat prickles up my neck. The scent of spearmint intermingled with a whisper of smoke is oddly intoxicating as he leans in at last, closing the space between us. His lips feel softer, fuller than I imagined—they brush gently against mine at first before crushing more firmly, melting as we fall into a harmonious rhythm. I shove my now flavorless gum into the hollow of my cheek, regretting my lack of foresight in not spitting it out but fearful that if

I stop now, the reality of the moment will break whatever spell holds me in his grasp. Our unified breath draws me deeper as the street vanishes around us, my mind a blank expanse save for one singular need. I abandon all passivity, all hope of feigning disinterest as he devours my mouth, and I pull him closer, his hands sliding down the length of my neck, thumbs tracing the line of my jaw with growing warmth and pressure.

The sudden peal of nearby laughter hits me like a bucket of ice-cold water. I break from our entwinement and turn to see a group of women piling into a car parked a few paces beyond the alleyway. I use the opportunity to spit out my hard, rubbery gum before I return my attention to Max, whose lips are now faintly tinged with my lipstick.

"I have to get back," I say, attempting to steady myself with deep, measured breaths. I reach out to rub away the color, but before I can withdraw my fingers, he catches me by the wrist, holding my gaze as he kisses the pad of my thumb softly.

"I know," he replies, releasing my hand as that slow, devilish smile spreads over his lips once more. "You have a date."

Walking beside Max, it feels as if the air between our bodies has become charged with static electricity—the hairs on my arms stand on end as the remnants of that kiss hang between us like sticky, invisible threads of spider silk. It's been so long—any comparison is a distant memory, but I know for a fact that I haven't felt that rising, feverish need in years. I find myself wondering how the strength of his hands would feel moving over other parts of me—how his lips would feel trailing my throat, my stomach, my thighs. Acting yet again as if he can hear my thoughts by some strange power, Max glances over with a knowing smile.

"Easy there," he says quietly, raising an eyebrow as I roll my eyes once more.

Just as we near the entrance to Bar Sperl, a tall figure rounds the far corner, clad in perfectly worn blue jeans with a suede jacket and beachy, shoulder-length hair. My blood runs cold as the man approaches, a look of recognition spreading over his face as he watches the two of us, his head slightly cocked to one side.

"Fuck. Me," I breathe as Max follows my gaze.

"Is that . . . ?"

I don't answer. It's clear to both of us that my date has arrived.

IV

Michael eyes Max curiously as the three of us stop just before the entryway. I instinctively step apart from my companion, hoping that I've done a good job of wiping the rosy hue from his lips as I force a nervous smile in greeting.

"Hey!" My voice cracks, and I feel like I'm moving through water as I swim forward, meeting Michael in a half hug. His presence feels dreamlike—as if he could disappear in a puff of smoke at any moment, returning the evening to the failure I'd only just accepted it to be. A flicker of movement catches my attention as Max shifts in place. *Not entirely a failure*, I think to myself, remembering the heat of the kiss that ended not two minutes ago.

"How's it going?" Michael says casually, still studying the scene with the faintest hint of scrutiny.

"Good, good!" I make a mental note to tone down my near-cartoonish enthusiasm, but every word I utter comes with all the phony exuberance of a waiter in pursuit of a good tip. "We just went to get some cigarettes—do you want one?"

I turn to Max expectantly, as if he can save me from myself, but he seems to be suppressing laughter.

"No—thanks," Michael replies with a pinch of salt before shifting his attention fully to Max. "I'm Michael, by the way."

Max steps up beside me, extending his hand with a broad, cheesy smile I haven't seen.

"I'm Max—really good to meet you! Shera's been on about you *all* night."

It takes everything in my power not to let my mouth fall open. Max seems to have shrunk in stature, his posture becoming almost apologetic as the signature devilish knit of his brow becomes a pleasant, welcoming archway. He's abandoned his natural lilting brogue and gritty, seductive demeanor, adopting the singsong intonation of a rather exaggeratedly posh English accent. In a single moment, it's as if he has transformed his physicality from that of a Svengali rockstar to a harmless admirer—my cheery, platonic confidant who would never be suspected of dirty dealings.

Michael accepts the faux Englishman's hand, introducing himself in kind as he shifts back into his usual look of unfazed ease.

"You gonna have a drink with us?"

"Oh, no, no, no!" Max shakes his head dramatically as he leaps back, hands crossed over his heart as if he fears offense. "I was simply keeping Shera company in your absence. We go way, *way* back but haven't had a chance to catch up in ages." He pauses as he turns to address me, placing a hand on my arm. His face remains fixed with a look of plastic cheer, but his middle finger traces small, pressured circles over my bicep, sending a secret shiver down my spine.

"It was *so* lovely running into you, darling. Please—*don't* be a stranger." He kisses me on both cheeks, his lips lingering for a moment more than a pleasant goodbye but not long enough to arouse true suspicion.

I half expect him to bow as he waves farewell before stepping around us and heading for the door. From my vantage point, looking just over Michael's shoulder, I watch as Max turns and winks at me one last time before disappearing inside.

"Shall we?" Michael asks with an easy smile as I stare up at him blankly. To my surprise, Max's absence has left me with a strange sense of emptiness—I can still feel his lips as the wind rushes past the wetness they left on my face.

"Yes," I blurt, wiping at my cheek with the heel of my palm. "Absolutely."

Inside, hordes of people now swarm the bar, but Michael's towering figure cuts through the crowd with relative ease. I stand behind him, feeling slight in comparison as he orders our drinks, and I scan the room for Lexi and Warren. My friends are nowhere to be seen—instead, we're met by a sea of keen-eyed women, many of whom appear to be appraising Michael. Even Nicole warms in his presence, the soft, foreign sound of her laugh ringing out in answer to whatever he just said.

"Let's go out back!" I shout over the cacophony of voices as Michael hands me my vodka soda. He nods in agreement.

As we step out onto the patio, the smell of cigarettes informs me that the owner of Bar Sperl is not battling his vices this week. Accordingly, the space is full of grateful smokers, standing and sitting in huddled flocks around the treelike patio heaters. It's slim pickings in the way of seating—the few weathered café chairs are already taken, with some people even perched on the rim of the wooden planter boxes lining the far wall.

As we head for a clearing in the center, I notice a line of three people talking among one another on a narrow bench. There, facing outward as if the whole of the patio is a show of theater in the round, sits Lexi, Warren, and Max King.

I feel my face reddening as Max pauses whatever story he's telling that has my friends laughing, just long enough to meet my gaze. I look away quickly, breathing steadily as I fight to return my attention to the tall, handsome man standing in front of me.

"How's your night been?" I ask earnestly, trying to focus intently on Michael despite Lexi's coat glowing in my periphery, a fiery orange beacon.

"Good. An old girlfriend of mine just moved into this gorgeous place looking out over Echo Park Lake—she was having a housewarming, so I was just chillin' there with a few friends." He pauses, sipping his old-fashioned and eyeing me curiously as if he's searching for some tell of a reaction.

"Must be nice to be on good terms with your ex like that," I reply sincerely.

"It is," Michael begins, running a hand through his long hair. "Riley and I have pretty much tailed each other from place to place for years—she's my best friend."

"Has that ever been . . . an issue with the women you've dated?"

Michael squints and tilts his head. It's a look that's become familiar—one that I realize gives him a striking resemblance to a cocker spaniel. "Not always—but I guess for the more insecure, jealous types it has. This one girl I was seeing before I moved kinda went crazy over it."

Insecure. Jealous. Crazy. He's approaching a full bingo card. I expect it to turn my stomach, but I find myself curiously inclined to dig deeper.

"And from your perspective, what makes a woman 'crazy'?"

He seems to be measuring his answer carefully, perhaps catching wind of what lies beneath the surface of my mildly inquisitive tone.

"Look, nothing's more important in a relationship than trust, right?" He pauses for confirmation, and I nod slowly. "This girl was obsessed with the idea that something was going on between Ry and me—she just couldn't let it go. I told her she needed to trust me, and she *said* she did. But if my phone went dead at Riley's, or I was out late and it happened to be with Riley, or the *one* time I had a few too many drinks and needed to crash on Riley's couch, she just got so controlling and *needy*."

Ding, ding, ding. The final deadly feminine sins—control and need. I try to maintain a look of neutrality as Michael continues his pitch.

"All I'm saying is, if you have self-esteem issues, that's *your* shit. You can't handle the presence of another beautiful woman in my life? That's not on me." His eyes become far off, his words more declarative, as if he's speaking directly to the ghost of his old flame. "This girl was *convinced* that Riley was, like, secretly still in love with me." He scoffs. "Total bullshit, and I told her so. She just wanted to keep me all to herself."

He takes a rushing, final swig of his drink, the ice cubes clinking violently against his teeth. Maybe it's the quick return of vodka to my system, or maybe Max's goading, pushing, provocative nature has rubbed off on me, but I suddenly feel an unfamiliar urge to challenge my date.

"Maybe it was less about Riley and more about you not making her feel safe."

Michael sucks his teeth, a shadow of anger flashing across his ever-easy countenance. He breathes deeply into the silence between us before fixing his face with an eerily serene smile.

"It wasn't my job to save her from her own delusions."

"*Delusions?*" I reply incredulously, forgetting myself as the blood rushes to my ears. "It sounds like you didn't like this girl very much to begin with—not enough to be sensitive to her feelings. This 'paranoid' anxiety she had just sounds like intuition. She knew you weren't invested in her—"

"I was at first," he interrupts. "I was drawn to her strength and independence, that's what I'm into—but I need someone who can hold their own in my world. It's like a pie chart that's split down the middle—half is devoted to my art, which always comes first, and the other part is my relationships as a whole, a mix of friends *and* romance. Riley's my creative partner and the lead in my film—she's a huge part of both categories, and this girl just couldn't accept that. I got tired of fighting."

I say nothing in response, busying myself with the soothing sensation of cold, wet glass against my skin. I picture Riley in my mind's eye—a woman worthy of a starring role in an arthouse masturbation film who finds any excuse to make physical contact with Michael as a subtle show of power. I imagine the mystery ex too—no doubt formidable in her own right, but weary. Her mind was made raw by the endless tug-of-war between what she knew in her soul and what she was told to believe. It's a possible, *probable* projection, but still . . .

"I bet she was tired too," I say finally.

"I'm sure she was." Michael sighs. "Being distrustful and self-pitying is exhausting. I tried to help, but at the end of the day, it was her trip—not mine. Have you ever read *The Four Agreements?* Maybe it's a cliché, but I've pretty much centered my whole philosophy around it—I mean, learning not to take anything personally totally changed my life . . ."

My vision blurs, and the edges of Michael's body fade as he continues to proselytize the gospel of spiritual bypass, the volume of his voice lowering as if issuing through a layer of drywall. My eyes wander back to the bench, just visible beyond Michael's hulking frame, and my heart sinks when I see that it's now occupied by a fresh crop of patrons.

"Sorry for going off on a tangent there," Michael says, his voice jolting back to full volume. His blue-green eyes twinkle as he smiles, and despite my irritation, I feel a small rush from being beneath his gaze.

"All good. I get it." Not entirely a lie—I understand perfectly. As an LA native, I'm well acquainted with the avoidant romantic to weaponized spiritual enlightenment pipeline.

"Alright, I gotta hit the head." Michael gently grabs my arms with both hands, bending his knees slightly as he does so and adopting a mocking, saccharine tone. "Will you be okay while I'm gone?"

I stare, mirroring him with a syrupy smile. "I'm a strong, independent woman—of course I will be."

Michael disappears inside, and I go for my phone immediately, finding four more messages from Lexi:

Told you he'd be here! Enjoy ;)

Wtf happened with Max? He says he doesn't "kiss and tell"

Warren and I are going to the Hollywood Hells party. Call if u need me. Love u.

*Hills party

I stare at the cloud-gray text bubbles. Yes, Michael is here. The victory I've longed for—the prize I've yearned for all these months is within my grasp. And yet there's a feeling of disappointment rising in my chest like floodwater from a basement.

A strong hand catches my waist, and the pressure of a warm body moves against my back.

"Quickly now, give me your number."

Max's voice is a low growl in my ear. I turn, trying to hide the elation on my face at the sight of him, but I can tell from the look on his that I haven't done a very good job. There's no time to feign protestation.

"Fine. Give me your phone."

When the deed is done, he smiles softly, leaning in to whisper, "I'll be seeing you, stranger," before he heads back into the bar. I stand there for what feels like ages, staring after him before Michael returns with a freshly half-drunk old-fashioned in his hand, his eyes apologizing before he even speaks.

"Hey, so I just got a call from the producer on my film—he wants to have an early meeting to go over some budget stuff. I'm sorry to cut this short, but—"

"No, no—I totally get it," I interrupt. "The art comes first. I'll walk you out."

Inside, the crowd has thinned some, and it's easier to spy the familiar faces peeking out from various nooks and crannies around the room. Much to my chagrin, Emily is still here, sandwiched between friends in a corner booth, watching as Michael and I make our tedious, awkward procession toward the door.

The night air rushes up to greet us as we exit Bar Sperl. Michael shoves his hands deep into his pockets as he faces me.

"Well, it was great to see you. Sorry again to run out on you like this."

"Don't worry about it—it was nice to see you too. I hope it doesn't take too long to get back to the canyon."

Michael rubs the back of his neck. "Yeah, it's usually not too bad this time of night, but my meeting's actually on this side of town tomorrow, so—"

I know what's coming before he even has a chance to say it. "Sleepover at Riley's?"

He chuckles ruefully. "Sleepover at Riley's."

Michael doesn't offer me a ride home, and I don't ask. He draws me into a warm, sturdy hug—the kind I previously lusted over but now only feel numb to.

"Let's do this again sometime—maybe dinner," he says, his voice reverberating through my cheek as it presses against his chest. For some reason, at those words, I find myself brimming with sadness again.

"Yeah, sounds great."

He breaks our embrace and says goodbye. I watch as he starts off down the street and even after he disappears from view.

I really can't blame Michael—that image of California cowboy chivalry was a shallow fantasy I painted on him myself. I stood there during each of our previous interactions, more concerned with imagining the curve of his muscular chest beneath those threadbare vintage tees than I ever was with his words. I built elaborate, secret worlds for us to share—filled with deep pleasures and simple joys, with long days in the sun and cold evenings by the fire. I wanted him to rescue me—to save me from Lexi's worry and Emily's mock sympathy. I wanted a shiny new trophy I could flaunt proudly as irrefutable evidence that I'm okay now. That I moved on.

I root around in my purse, my hand instantly drawing to my phone like a magnet. It's 11:02 p.m.—two hours to the minute since I arrived.

I consider joining Warren and Lexi—a party could be a good distraction, but then again, it would, in all likelihood, be a night I have lived before and have never really enjoyed. Standing around watching desperate people work the room, vying for a taste of fame adjacency, and cozying up to the glassy-eyed children of waning celebrities would be more painful than entertaining. No—better to just go home; take a long, hot shower; sleep until the sun sits high in the sky like a runny, golden yoke; and then sleep some more.

I open the Uber app and begin typing in my address, but before I can finish, a text from an unknown number appears on the screen.

Look up.

Instinctively, I don't obey right away. Instead, I survey my immediate surroundings with caution, having fallen asleep to far too many hours of *Law & Order: Special Victims Unit* to ever rule out the possibility of abduction. My phone buzzes again.

Across the road.

I follow instructions this time, my pulse quickening as I turn my attention to the black Lincoln Navigator parked across the way. It flashes its high beams twice as I watch and wait, making no motion toward it. The rear door swings open, seemingly in invitation, as my phone vibrates once more.

Come back to mine.

My stomach becomes a fluttering mess as I look up to see Max emerging from the car, phone in hand. He flashes a wide grin as he brandishes the device—the tool with which he's set his cunning trap, and I can't help but smile back, shaking my head in disbelief.

My fingers move to my hand necklace, my thumb gliding over the calming, familiar shape of it. I can't be certain what led us to this moment, whether it's fate or an elaborate scheme. I don't know what I want from him, from someone who probably won't have anything more to give me than a memory—a moment in time. I can't be sure what will happen if I follow him down the rabbit hole, where it will lead, and whether or not I'll be better for it or worse—but at this moment, I don't care to know the end of the story. As Max looks on, I lift my phone and type out my reply.

Let's go.

V

"The car's a little much, don't you think?" I ask as I heave myself into the large luxury SUV Uber.

"Well, that depends," he replies, sliding into a sidesaddle position, his back against the far door. "Are you impressed?"

His broad grin is infectious—I bite my lip as the car starts off on its way, hurtling down Sunset Boulevard, past bars and side streets, dark cafés and late-night street meat stands. As it all blurs past my window, the reality of my vulnerable position begins to dawn on me, diminishing the surge of confidence that inspired my whimsical impulsivity.

"So, where do you live?"

"I'm actually in an Airbnb at the moment. Been doing that for some time now while I look for a permanent place." He pauses, sensing my faint apprehension. "Don't worry, it's close by—just above the reservoir."

Good, I think to myself, nodding with a rush of relief. In all likelihood, this is not a kidnapping, but if it is, at least I'll know my surroundings well enough. Still, when Max's phone buzzes, I seize the opportunity to text Lexi.

Going to Max's place. You have my location.

I'll call you tomorrow.

My phone has barely dimmed when it begins vibrating over and over again, as if to a beat. I don't bother to check.

"Robert," Max leans forward, raising his voice as he addresses the driver, "could you pull in at the liquor shop coming up there?"

There's a pause. I imagine Robert has endured a good deal of Max's requests already. "No problem, sir," he replies with the whisper of a midwestern accent.

"Good man!" Max exclaims as the car veers into the parking lot.

Fearing the internal spiral that's sure to come if I'm left alone with my thoughts, I follow Max inside, lazily perusing the shelves while he moves through the store with purpose. As I scan the stacks of top ramen and dusty boxes of cereal, the store door chimes repeatedly, and I look up to see three young women step inside. They're all beautiful and dressed to the nines, bare midriffs and short hems accentuating their stunning figures as they tumble inside, giggling and murmuring among one another. My face flushes as they fan out like a pod of sirens, moving toward where Max stands studying a bottle of red wine.

The fairest of them all, a towering brunette with curtain bangs, brown skin, and full breasts barely concealed within a thin white tube top, is the first to catch sight of Max, that now-familiar look of recognition crossing her face. I hold my breath as she steps beside him and examines a bottle of the same label. When he finally notices his admirer, Max does a slight double take, requiring only a millisecond to run his eyes over the length of her. She smiles as their gazes meet, and he smiles back—though it's not the same one he's shown me throughout the night. It's almost

46

courteous—like the sort one flashes when passing a fellow hiker on the trail.

I've all but melted into the shelf behind me by the time Max makes his way to the cash wrap, leaving the tittering women in his wake as they reconvene. I try to look busy, committed to finding whatever imaginary thing I'm looking for, as Max directs the clerk to pull a bottle of Grey Goose in addition to the cabernet he selected. The women are watching. Whatever prior mission urged the trio into the store has been abandoned. They're hunting now.

"Do you need anything?" Max's voice cuts through my dark trance as he turns, prompting the women's heads to snap toward me too.

"All good," I chirp sheepishly, my eyes still fixed on the cornucopia of snacks before me. I peek just long enough to see a look of curiosity cross Max's face—as if he feels my changing energy through the ether. When I glance at the women, the brunette's eyes are unflinching—maybe even challenging as they bore into mine. Still, she offers a small, polite smile, and I return one tightly.

The clerk hands Max the plastic bag of provisions as I move swiftly for the door, making a beeline for the car. I don't turn to see if my companion is in tow—the sound of clinking bottles behind me serves as evidence enough.

"Hi, *so* sorry to bother you," comes the slight rasp of a sultry voice at my back. I turn in unison with Max to see the tall brunette, her shapely, exposed legs and arms dotted with raised goose bumps. The chilly air has also hardened the points of her nipples, and I try not to stare as they poke prominently through the thin fabric of her top.

"I wouldn't normally do this, but I'm a *huge* fan," she gushes, her friends standing just behind her.

"Oh, yeah?" Max chuckles. "Sounds like you've got woeful taste."

The girl tilts her head slightly as his self-effacing joke takes a moment to work itself through her. When it lands, she laughs to herself cooly, flashing a flirtatious smile before pulling the strap of her pointlessly miniature baguette purse over her shoulder and tucking a lock of sleek hair behind her ear.

"How long are you in town for?" she asks daringly.

"I live here now, so, forever, I suppose," he replies, still open-faced and warm. "I'm looking for a house at the moment, actually—you wouldn't happen to know a good estate agent, would you?"

Max's banter falls flat against her as another beat passes before she laughs again. "Oh, no. I don't—but if you need a tour guide to show you around, I'm sure I can help." She pauses, glancing toward me. "As long as your . . . friend doesn't mind."

A *tour guide*? First of all, she's stolen my line, but more importantly—*friend*? Max chuckles again, softly now, as if he's only now realizing her intentions.

"Ah, you're too kind."

She looks down at her feet as if overcome by sudden shyness, though her hubris belies the gesture. "So, do you have a girlfriend?"

I want nothing more than to disappear, to run as far from the scene as possible, but I stand rooted, my feet leaden as I burn with humiliation. Even before everything happened, I didn't do well with the idea of competition. I suppose I cling to a romantic notion that anyone worth having will simply choose me—that I won't have to challenge all the pretty girls in Los Angeles to a Greco-Roman wrestling match of forward flirtation and win a man's affection by being the last one standing. I'm sure Lexi would say it's my "self-esteem issue"—that I don't feel comfortable making space for myself. Maybe she's right.

I run the tape, trying to decide if it's more dignified to call my own car and stand waiting as their romance unfolds or just set off walking in the direction of my apartment.

Max doesn't look at me—his face is unreadable as he runs a hand through his shaggy hair and asks the woman, "What's your name?"

"Sonia," she answers quickly as all three seem to hold their breath in unison.

I feel like I'm going to be sick. I didn't want to acknowledge Max's celebrity, but maybe that was my mistake—I should know that in this city especially, those rich in social currency are considered "up for grabs" to anyone with the courage to approach. Maybe if I wasn't so rough around the edges, if I was accepting of his advances like a doe-eyed fan, he would choose me instead. Maybe if I didn't hide myself in layers of black—from this vantage point, probably modest to the point of *sexlessness*—Sonia wouldn't take one look at me and assume I'm just a friend—or at least, someone who won't stand in her way. Or maybe I could've saved myself the trouble altogether if I just kept fucking walking when he tried to speak to me at the bar. If I never gave him the time of day, never fell under the spell of his masterful charm or had a taste of what smoldered so mysteriously between us, I wouldn't be standing here now paying the price—

49

"Sonia," Max repeats warmly, "I don't have a girlfriend." He turns, moving beside me as he places a hand between my shoulder blades. "However—*this* is my wife."

I stand speechless as the woman's face floods with a mix of surprise and disappointment. Max pokes the small of my back softly, and I understand the gesture as a quiet encouragement to play along. Invigorated with relief, I oblige, smiling with as much sincerity as I can muster.

"I'm—Cora Bittering."

It's the first name that comes to mind—the space colonist housewife from "Dark They Were, and Golden-Eyed." Max glows with pride as he looks at me. I want to kiss him, but my still-lingering bitterness from watching him entertain Sonia's advances urges my role-play in a different direction. I shove him without warning—the force is minimal, but he still stumbles back, the bottles clinking as utter bewilderment replaces his pride.

"Max, what the *fuck?* We haven't even told our families yet, and you're sharing all our business with complete *strangers?*"

He quickly catches on, collecting himself as he puts up his hands in defense. "I'm sorry, sweetheart, I just can't contain myself." His face is sorrowful, heavy with remorse. "I have the most beautiful, brilliant wife in the world, and I don't care who knows it!"

I sigh heavily and turn to the women, still standing before us with faces reflecting varying degrees of confusion. "Sonia, right?" I address her directly. "We *just* eloped and hoped to keep it secret for a little while." I pause, glancing at Max, who's now hanging on my every word, waiting to hear what I'll say next. "I won't bore you with all the details, but our families *hate* each other. My cousin, in particular, is crazy—he's basically out for blood, and it's just continued to escalate. He even baited Max's best friend into an actual *physical* fight over it recently—"

I wonder for a moment if I've gone too far as I strain to remember all the convoluted plot points of *Romeo and Juliet* that I can apply to this improv scene. Judging from Sonia's look of vague skepticism, as if she can sense some untruth but can't figure out what it is exactly, I figure it's better to quit while I'm ahead.

"Bottom line, we would appreciate it if you kept this private," I conclude, drawing my eyebrows in a performance of deep concern.

A beat passes as the trio glances between us, dismay and annoyance apparent on their pretty faces.

"Um—yeah, sure," Sonia says finally.

Max exhales dramatically. "Oh, thank you, Sonia! You've kept a very sorry man from the doghouse tonight." He puts his arm around my shoulders as we begin to back away. "And thank you for being a fan—please keep listening." I climb into the car as he continues to shout from outside, even though the women have turned away. "Keep streaming, buy tickets, buy our merch! Please—I must keep my new bride in pearls and finery!"

Max tumbles in beside me and shuts the door as the car starts on its way again. He watches me curiously, studying my face as if he's trying to ascertain some new piece of me that was previously hidden.

"Well, well, well. Quite a performance, Ms. Bittering," he says evenly as I bow my head slightly. I can't help my smile—I'm high on the fun of it, the exhilaration of matching wits and succeeding.

"I should say the same to you, Mr. King—or is that King-Bittering?" He raises an eyebrow slightly as I continue. "Sorry, I don't plan on taking your last name, so maybe we'll both hyphenate."

His eyes gleam. "So you do know who I am?"

Shit. He never told me his full name. The hilarity dies on my face, replaced by a burning scarlet flush. "No—not before tonight. My friend Warren told me, but that's not why I'm—"

"Easy, Shera," Max interrupts. "I know you're not here because of that." He knits his fingers behind his head and leans against the headrest in a look of ultimate playboy repose. "If you were, I wouldn't have had to do all that song and dance to get you to come back with me." I shoot him a look, and he winks.

"I believe you. *Sonia* made that abundantly clear," I mutter, crossing my legs as I turn my attention to the window.

"Oh no." Max, still unbuckled, slides closer to me. "Am I sensing a bit of the green-eyed monster?" Satisfaction drips from every word, but I say nothing. He clicks his tongue teasingly.

"I'm not jealous," I say tightly. "I just found it disrespectful. She didn't even consider that I could be—you know. It was just a competition she wanted to win."

"And would you have competed?"

"What?"

His jesting tone is gone as he watches me with measured sincerity. "Would you have fought, or would you have flown?"

Aside from the rumbling tires and the slight whistling sound from Robert's nostrils whenever he exhales, the car feels tensely quiet. I sense we're winding up into the hillside above the Silver Lake Reservoir now, though the outside world has become pitch black through the tinted windows, interrupted only by the occasional orange glow of streetlamps. Max's face is earnest in the dim light as he waits for my reply—as if the answer will provide him with some assurance he longs for.

"I don't care enough to compete," I announce, my words ringing through the silence.

Max shifts back into his seat, sighing. "Well, Sonia did seem pretty eager to show me around," he remarks, returning to his casual bravado. "If you don't care, maybe we should turn around. She seemed like a nice girl—"

"*Don't* do that," I snarl, and he stops cold, his face softening into something like concern. "Don't pit me against another woman in any scenario—real or imagined."

Max looks me up and down for a moment, his face unreadable. I try to hold firm, but a small part of me worries I went too far—while another wonders why I gave him a piece of my mind at all.

"Understood. On my honor, as your loyal husband, I swear it'll never happen again." He places a hand over his heart, his small, genuine smile urging me to soften.

"And for the record, you're not giving me much credit." He lifts his swearing hand and raises a finger. "There was a time, to be sure, when I'd jump into bed with any pretty girl who told me she was a fan, but I'm older and wiser now. These days, I'm not easily seduced by flattery. I like a good bit of banter . . ." He stares plainly at my mouth. "You know, someone who's a bit of a challenge."

I consider his words before replying, "Who said I was getting anywhere near your bed?"

He smirks, seemingly relieved that I've returned to our biting swordplay. "Bed, table, floor, balcony railing." He pauses, his eyes smoldering as they bore into me. "It's all the same."

The electric pulse between my legs at these last words is unexpected. I swallow hard as Max watches me, clearly enjoying the minor disruption he caused. I look away, busying myself with a hard ridge of stitching on the seat beneath me.

"You feeling alright?" Max probes, feigning concern as he leans toward me. "You're looking a bit rosy . . ." The back of his hand is at my brow before I can stop it—cool against the warmth radiating from me.

"Fine, thanks." I swat him away as he grins. Something within me doesn't mind the teasing—the minor torment of his effect on me and the satisfaction he relishes as a result.

"Here we are," Robert's soft voice interrupts from the front seat as we roll to a stop.

"Grand. Thank you, Robert."

It's deathly quiet as we step out onto the street before a low, '70s-style stilt house. With steely gray stucco and a small patch of succulents out front, it isn't much to look at from the outside, but as we walk through the covered carport toward the entryway, I glimpse the moonlit shadows of furniture that fill a large interior through the glass door panel. Max taps the numbers on the entry pad, but the handle remains locked.

"Can never remember the fucking code," he mutters to himself. "Hold this for a moment, will you?"

He hands me the liquor store haul as he grabs his phone, one handle falling in the transfer between us. As the bag gapes open, I spy a box of Trojan condoms, glowing orange amid the black plastic and tinkering glass. My stomach somersaults. I didn't notice him buying them, and the fact that he did feels like a green flag, but . . . but the reality of the situation—the reason I came here strikes me hard as I stare down at the packaging. What else had I imagined I was coming home with him for? We're going to have *sex*. I'm going to take off my clothes and reveal myself to this man. I'm going to be with another person intimately for the first time since—

"*Finally.*"

The keypad beeps, followed by a mechanical whirring as Max opens the door, taking the bag from me as he steps inside and flicks on the lights.

I stop at the threshold like a vampire who requires an invitation. The evening's events suddenly feel surreal. A few short hours ago, I was sick with a different fantasy, and now I feel . . . nothing at the thought of it. I wanted Michael so badly—or at least, I thought I did. I *am* disappointed that nothing came of our date, but somehow it feels like the disappointment of flunking an interview for a job I never wanted to begin with. Maybe Max is the right job.

I stand puzzling over what exactly I've assigned the analogy of a "job" to mean when Max's voice breaks through my quiet contemplation.

"Coming?"

My host stands waiting for me with a warm, comforting smile. Again, that fated feeling sweeps my mind and body blank—no apprehension or anxiety, only his face driving me toward whatever lies ahead as I step inside and close the door.

VI

The place is far homier than I expected, with evidence of Max's long-haul stay apparent in the paper-strewn workspace that has taken over the large, beautiful dining room. He busies himself as he walks ahead of me, gathering empty cups and plates, remnants of takeout, and a crumpled black sweater lying in our path as I move dreamily toward the living room. Approaching the floor-to-ceiling windows flanking a large painted brick fireplace, I take in the unobstructed view of the Silver Lake Reservoir, paying special attention to the balcony deck and that perimeter railing Max mentioned back in the car.

"Sorry," my host says, slightly breathless, as he appears beside me. "Haven't had company in a little while."

"It's fine—it's a gorgeous house."

Max nods. "I'm lucky." He turns, looking back toward the room. "Well, make yourself at home. Would you like a drink?"

"Yes," I blurt so quickly he starts with the rush of it.

Max returns to the kitchen, and I make my way to the curved, rust-colored sectional. Several long minutes pass as I stare up at the wall clock ticking in perfect time with my heartbeat:

11:38 p.m.—not that it matters. I don't know why I'm still keep-ing track like I'm waiting for something. All it's doing now is reminding me that I chose to accompany a strange man home at a late hour—and that I still don't know how I feel about it.

A faint, familiar melody reaches my ears as the slow-building intro of "Glory Box" by Portishead plays from unseen speakers. Max appears with two generous glasses of wine, handing one over as he takes a seat beside me and raises his.

"To endless possibilities," he says, staring into my eyes as our glasses meet with a soft *clink*. I nod and sip, wondering for a moment if he heard Lexi's toast back at Bar Sperl or if, like many other strange things this evening, it's purely coincidental.

"So . . ." Max takes a long drink from his glass as he settles in beside me. "Tell me about your date."

"Must we?" I groan like a petulant child, eliciting a smirk from him. When he only stares over the rim of his glass but says nothing else, I sigh, "It doesn't matter. I think that chapter's over for me."

Max's eyes gleam with curiosity as he studies me. "Did he try to get you back to his place?"

"Far from it," I snort. "I don't think he likes me." I pause, the words coming to me in real time. "But more importantly, I don't think I like *him*. I guess he just—didn't live up to the fantasy."

Max smiles somewhat triumphantly as he places his glass on the coffee table. "Well, I could've told you that."

"Oh, is that so?" I sneer, raising my eyebrows.

"It is," he says matter-of-factly. "There were signs."

"Such as?"

He leans in conspiratorially. "Well, for starters, you were wet for me from the moment I said hello. If you'd been into him, you wouldn't have been so easily distracted."

My heart skips a beat, and I feel myself turn scarlet at Max's words, hit with another pulsing electric shock. I set my glass beside his, readying for a biting rebuttal.

"That is not true, and you know it. If anything, you were *unrelentingly* annoying. You just kept popping up everywhere and . . ."

I don't have a chance to finish my sentence. My words vanish at the sudden sensation of his hand sliding over my knee, gliding slowly, firmly, as he moves up my leg like a snake. I hold my breath, remaining perfectly still as I watch his face—expressionless, vacant. His eyes trail the pathway of his hand, his thumb moving over my inner thigh, brushing dangerously close as my blood turns fiery.

"See?" he says quietly, clinically. "Look how easy it is for me to distract you now."

I'm not sure who strikes first, but in a flash, his mouth is on mine, his free hand grasping the side of my neck as the other moves between my legs. Pressure turns to aching need as his fingers circle through the barrier of my thin slacks, and I lift my hips to meet him.

"Take this off," he demands softly, tugging at my blazer as I shrug it from my shoulders and toss it to the floor.

I feel myself slipping sideways, down and down as I come to rest fully reclined on the sofa, with Max's body hovering over mine. He leans down, trailing slow, hungry kisses along my neck and up my jaw before he finds my mouth again, his tongue gently parting my lips as it enters. My own hands remain oddly passive, some part of me still frozen in disbelief. Every sensation feels both completely new and reminiscent of times I remember hazily now, as if from a distant dream.

A sudden tugging sensation below my navel cuts through the haze of euphoria as I realize his fingers have found the buckle of my belt—

Too soon, my mind barks as I feel the prong slip from its hole.

This is it, the moment I imagined a thousand times for almost a year—the thing I need to do, like ripping off a Band-Aid, and yet—

Too soon, the mental warning bell rings out again as I feel the leather dragging through my belt loops.

Maybe I was so focused on getting here, on treating sex like some merit badge I can earn to prove I'm still desirable, that I never fully considered how it would make me feel. Maybe I'm not ready—

"Wait!" I squeak as he rises up to look at me. "I—I need to know you better."

"What?"

"I need more time, more information—I don't know where you're from or if you have siblings or if you've ever *actually* been married or have children or—if you're . . . allergic to shellfish."

Max remains positioned above me as he searches my face. Having hit the brakes at such a critical moment, I expect disappointment, anger even, but he seems to be fighting the urge to laugh.

"You are an odd one, Shera."

"I'm serious! I don't do this very often, and I—we need to know each other for me to feel comfortable."

I hold my breath, both grateful for his mild reaction and a

little disappointed to lose the heat of his touch. He studies my face a moment longer before leaning down to kiss me once on the tip of my nose.

"Dublin, a sister, a fiancée but never tied the knot, and not that I'm aware of," Max replies.

"No children that you're aware of or—not sure if you're allergic?"

"Both." He grins devilishly, and I gently shove him away.

After some straightening of garments, we both right ourselves on the sofa again. I reach for my wine and take a long draft as Max chuckles beside me.

"You know, you don't have to be nervous—it's no bother at all that you wanted to stop," he assures me. He's right, of course, but it's only taken a handful of spiteful words and pressuring hands over the years to make me question it.

"I mean it—I get off on you enjoying yourself. There's no pleasure in it for me at your expense," he insists with a look of deep, meaningful sincerity that sets my heart aflutter. I nod as he reaches for his glass. "So, how should we get to know each other then?"

I consider the question, drawing inspiration from memories of teen slumber parties and summer camp initiations. "I'll ask you something, and then you can ask me. We can both choose to skip, but only twice."

He nods, his eyes twinkling. "Alright then—but I want to go first."

I raise my glass in a gesture of concession as he squints, scanning in search of inspiration.

"Where'd you go to school?"

"Next question."

Max cocks his head. "Why?"

"It's boring," I declare.

"*Jesus.*" He sighs dramatically, and I smirk, enjoying the long *a* sound when his accent curls around the soft expletive. "You're not gonna make this easy, are you?" He runs a hand over his chin in contemplation. "Okay, fine—who'd you lose your virginity to?"

I smile as the memory swims into my mind. "Seiji Tanaka—he was a Japanese exchange student who was being hosted by my mom's best friend." I pause, recalling the details of what now feels like someone else's life. "We were both sixteen, and there was a slight language barrier, but we had this tense flirtation—I still don't know if anyone ever found out. We just snuck into the home office at a family party and did it right there on the rug. It was over before anyone even noticed we were gone."

"Stop the *lights.*" Max gasps teasingly. "And I thought you were a nice girl."

"Okay, my turn," I say, enjoying the game already. "Tell me about your music."

"Now *that's* boring," Max snorts, taking a hefty swig of wine.

"I'm not asking what it's like to be recognized on the street or what your thoughts are on the future of the industry," I retort. "I want to know about your music. I've never even heard any of it." He laughs at this, curiosity slowly returning.

"Well, I sing, play guitar, and write most of the music. It's sort of postpunk, punk rock, I don't know." He pauses as I give a rolling hand gesture for him to continue, but he only shrugs.

"Your band's called Dog from Hell?"

He nods, running his free hand over his chin. "Yeah, it's,

um—it's from the title of a book I loved growing up—*Love Is a Dog from Hell*."

"I remember that one. Bukowski."

Max closes his eyes, shaking his head. "I know it's a cliché. I'm a bit scarlet at the name now, but that's what happens when you start a band young." He huffs a small laugh. "It's been over ten years now, so I suppose we're stuck with it."

"Look, we can't help what inspires us. I think we all have this instinct to hate on what we loved, especially in our youth—judging ourselves before someone else has a chance to." I shake my head, my own clandestine artistic attachments coming to mind. "But I don't know, I think that's kind of . . . sad." He nods again, his eyes roving my face with a note of intrigue that sends my pulse jumping. "Like it or not, that book was meaningful to you at one time—I'm sure whatever it sparked had a hand in bringing you to where you are now."

"Fair enough." He smiles, a glimmer of genuine gratitude or maybe relief flashing behind his eyes.

Before I can press him further, Max begins his own interrogation. "So, what's your thing?"

The question sinks low in my belly, but I prepare my script anyway.

"I write opinion pieces for a few magazines when I can, and I fill the gaps in my income with freelance copywriting—like marketing, ads. Boring stuff." I shrug.

"Now you've answered the question 'What do you do for money?' but that's not what I asked."

I watch him, ruminating on his genuine, inquisitive nature.

The way he asks not for the sake of asking but for the sake of truth.

"My 'thing' is writing. I'm a writer."

"And what do you write?"

"Well, not much lately besides what I do for money." I laugh ruefully. "But I was working on a novel for a while. I'd actually finished it, but then I scrapped the ending and set it aside last year."

"A novel? As in, a *book?*" Max raises his eyebrows incredulously.

It dawns on me that in all those months, I never divulged this information to Michael—in fact, what exactly we spoke about at all besides general musings about Los Angeles and his own art and ambition was a blank expanse in my memory. He never asked about my passions, and I was so busy trying to show my interest in him that I never offered. Looking back, I'm not sure which is the greater sin—his lack of interest or my lack of self-assertion.

I let myself bask in the glow of Max's admiration, smiling as he asks, "What's it about?"

"It's a love story about two people who find themselves sharing the same dreams every night. In their dream world, they fall for each other and build this whole magical life together, so when they finally meet by chance, it feels like this big, fated, beautiful thing."

It's an effort to rack my brain, trying to recall the story I abandoned as a casualty of my lost inspiration—the grief-induced writer's block that all but robbed me of my greatest passion. Max is raptly attentive as I slow, remembering.

"But as they explore their relationship in the real world, they both realize they're actually only in love with the dream versions of each other—in reality, she's this vindictive, conniving con woman, and he's a selfish, arrogant freeloader."

"You call that a love story?" Max teases. "So, what's the new ending?"

"I'm not sure yet. Originally, they realize that while it doesn't look the way it did in their dream world, they're still perfectly matched as their true, kind of horrible selves. They're a couple of misfit hustlers, flawed and broken—they're mirrors of each other. But when I had it all written out, it just didn't feel plausible—the idea that they would recognize that and wouldn't just tear each other apart." I pause, considering. "Realistically, one of them probably kills the other."

Max's sharp, hearty laugh is infectious, and I find myself joining him. "I believe it was Oscar Wilde who said, 'Life imitates art.' Let's hope he was wrong about that one," he replies with a mocking, wary look.

We volley back and forth for some time, imbibing all the while until only the dregs of the bottle remain, my vision becoming pleasantly blurred at the edges. Among other things, Max reveals a clandestine fascination with American trash TV, a deathly fear of mice, and that the star of his first wet dream was Grace Jones. I find myself enjoying being bound by the rules that force me to answer—even when sharing my more innocuous truths, it feels oddly exciting.

After Max learns that my childhood pet was a gerbil named Puck, and he shares that his favorite guilty pleasure film is *Under the Tuscan Sun*, it's his turn again. I sit, still giggling over his earnest explanation that Diane Lane just "does something to him" as he says, "Now tell me about your last relationship."

My laughter evaporates. I consider skipping, but I draw in a steadying breath and prepare my measured words. "We were together for three years, broke up nearly a year ago now."

"His name?" he asks softly, his gaze steady, searching.

"Elliot."

The sound of it feels foreign in my mouth, weighted and strange, like the pronunciation of a language I once spoke but hardly remember now. Max nods knowingly as his eyes move over me, resting on my lips and chest. Something in his gentle smile tells me that he knows I've been broken and remade—that I'm still fragile and not ready to be pressed.

"I won't pry, but I will say something I said before." He reaches forward, moving a single braid behind my shoulder. "He's a fool."

"I guess that's my type," I reply, laughing ruefully as I lean my head against the sofa.

"Present company excluded, I hope?" His cheeky smile has returned.

"You're something else entirely." I tilt my head, feigning contemplation. "You remind me of a court jester—a *literal* fool."

"That's fair. I wish I could disagree about your bad judgment, but I've seen it with my own eyes," Max teases, clearly trying to return to a spirit of levity.

"Oh god, give it a rest!" I groan again at the mention of what now feels like an entirely separate evening from this one.

"I'm serious!" Max exclaims. "I played it cool earlier, but—what the *fuck* did you see in Michael?" His tone is surprisingly explosive—as if he was sitting on the words now rushing out in an unstoppable torrent. "He's good-looking, I suppose, but an absolute *dryshite*, to be sure. He's just not—not *you* at all."

I watch him in slight disbelief, eyes narrowed, my mouth opening and closing uselessly like a fish on land as his rant continues, fueled by the ease we developed over the course of that bottle.

"I mean, listen, we all get lonely sometimes. I understand the feeling of wanting a little attention—"

"You don't know what you're talking about." I spit the words, sitting bolt upright. "It wasn't about 'attention' for the sake of my ego. I was attracted to him, and yeah, I ignored the signs that he's kind of a tool, but I wanted to feel like someone actually wanted me—"

"How is that not the same thing?" Max crows as my blood reaches a boiling point.

"Because it wasn't about some surface-level vanity bullshit—I *needed* to fuck him!" His jeering, goading smile falters at my snapping words and sudden shift. "Or—or maybe I didn't! I don't know—maybe I told myself I wanted to and fixated for four months on a guy whose interest in me was lukewarm at best because deep down, I knew nothing would happen."

Max looks slightly perplexed, his brow furrowing as his tone turns remorseful. "Shera, I'm—"

"And you know what, maybe you're right!" I can feel my voice cracking unexpectedly. "I wanted to feel desired and *chosen*. I wanted someone to make me feel good about myself because—" *Nope—keep it together.* I stop myself, pushing the cottony stuffing of inner turmoil back inside and zipping myself tightly. These are thoughts I didn't let myself *think* until now, let alone say—and why am I saying them to him? "Whatever—the point is, you have *no* right to judge me for something you don't even understand and—"

Max interrupts, grasping my shoulders urgently as if sensing my need to be steadied.

"Shera, I was being a prick, and I'm truly sorry." His hands slide down to my forearms. "Look, meeting your man Michael and watching his way with you—I could just tell he's right up himself." He looks away for a moment, considering his words. "I mean, you're stunning—you stunned me when I first saw you, but it's more than that. You're clever and thoughtful and—" His eyes return, burning into mine as my body warms. "I suppose I just couldn't understand your interest in him."

I consider that this could be empty flattery, a way to appease me, but as I search his face, I find that now-familiar sincerity.

"I really didn't mean to have a go at you like that before—it isn't my place, to be sure," he continues, his thumbs brushing over my skin softly as he continues to hold my arms. "Of course you deserve to feel desired and chosen—but I also believe you deserve to be *seen*."

It's true—Michael didn't see me. I was so hell-bent on my mission to get back on the horse, to date and fuck and whatever else in the hopes that I could will myself to be okay again, that I didn't even notice. In fact, I refused to really see him either.

My hackles lower as Max's words sink in. Meeting his unwavering gaze, a feeling settles over me—spreading with the heat of his hands and filling my entire being. Suddenly, as if moved by some invisible force, I find myself standing up quietly, breathing hard as he watches me pull my turtleneck over my head and drop it to the floor. Then I reach for the once-off-limits buckle, removing the belt and letting my pants fall with it as I step beside the crumpled heap. Max's face takes an odd expression—both knowing and uncertain. I swallow hard as I undo the clasp of my simple black bra, the slight chill hardening my nipples.

Before I can proceed, Max rises and steps toward me, his eyes holding mine despite my nudity. He doesn't move, even while I remove my underwear with trembling hands, exhaling sharply as I reveal the totality of my body to him.

"*Stunning*," he murmurs, taking a short step toward me as his mouth hovers just a hair's breadth from mine.

My own breath catches in my lungs at the sensation of his hand slowly gliding from my wrist to the sharp curve of my shoulder, winding up and up in a serpentine motion again as it did before. I don't dare move a muscle—his fingers sweep over my collarbones, fanning outward as his palm moves to my breast, thumb caressing the soft skin there before inching down. The muscles of my stomach flutter as his touch trails fire, and my heartbeat thunders in my ears. I want to beg, to plead for him to keep going toward the smoldering heat between my legs, but I stay silent as he pauses just below my navel.

"I hope you know me well enough now," he says finally, breathing heavily with the effort of his restraint.

"I do." I swallow.

The words have barely left my lips when his fingers finally hit home, sinking into me slowly as my breath stops short.

"Good," he says, a faint smile tucked behind his eyes. "I think it's my turn to know you."

VII

The drumbeat of my heart rattles through my entire body as Max leads me down a narrow hallway to the bedroom. The warm-wooded space, illuminated only by the dim light of a sculptural paper lantern, seems to breathe in unison with us as we enter. In contrast to the haphazardly strewn odds and ends in the rest of the house, the California king has been carefully made, the green linen duvet smooth beneath freshly fluffed pillows, all piled upright against the wooden headboard.

Once inside, Max turns to me, this time allowing himself to study my body as the unbridled, lustful blaze within his eyes turns animalistic. His kiss is deeper than before—familiar now in a way that eases my nerves as one hand travels to my waist and the other trails lightly along the curve of my spine, fingers walking vertebra by vertebra, down and down. Emboldened by need, I pull at the hem of his thin black sweater, moving the fabric up and over his head to reveal a surprising physique—lean and muscled like a Grecian statue. My eyes catch the inky black mark of a tattoo above his heart, a time-worn cursive scrawl spelling out the word *Catríona*. I ponder the name for only a moment as his hands begin moving over my ass, kneading firmly, almost roughly, as they urge me back to the present, and I busy myself with the button of his pants.

When Max is down to his Calvin Klein boxer briefs, I back away, reclining slowly on the bed in waiting. Desire again outpaces my timidity—I crave the petal softness of his lips on my skin, the strength of his hands, and the weight of his body over mine with every fiber of my being. At last, he digs his thumbs into the waistband of his underwear, revealing his considerable size and length—another welcome surprise, although he remains noticeably soft.

He moves to me, his warmth sliding over my body, enveloping me. When his hand brushes my thigh, it's almost too much to bear—I try to angle my hips, urging his fingers to return to their previous sheath, but he grips the soft flesh instead, stopping both of our movements as he lets out a low laugh.

"*Please*," I whimper breathlessly as he kisses my neck.

"Please what?" He moves closer, his tone firm and direct, like that of a teacher asking a student to speak up and enunciate.

I say nothing, overpowered by the command of his presence, aching with my own need, and yet . . . still unable to surrender completely to him.

"Do you want me to touch you?" His breath is hot in my ear as I writhe almost imperceptibly beneath him.

Max doesn't wait for an answer as he gives me what he knows I want. A soft moan escapes my lips, but his mouth devours it hungrily as my leg hooks around his body, drawing him closer still. The fluidity of his motion tells me just how slick I am as his fingers work into me, deep and shallow, coaxing and turning, teasing endlessly. The sensation floods my brain as I move against him on instinct, my own fingers winding into his dark hair. I need more—I need all of him. I slide my hand down, feeling him for the first time, warm and soft against my fingers—

Still soft? A small seed of worry works its way into my mind as I freeze and look into his eyes, a mutual awareness reflected there.

"I-Is everything—okay?" I stammer as cooly as I can muster. Max sighs heavily and withdraws his fingers, the horrible emptiness of his retreat paling in comparison to the humiliation creeping through me.

"It's fucking fantastic." He rises up, sitting back on his heels, his hands still resting on my thighs. "But unfortunately, that message doesn't always get delivered."

I prop myself up on my elbows and instinctually knock my knees together in a small effort to conceal myself. I know, of course, that there's a difference between intellectual and carnal attraction—those times when the mind says yes while the body remains unresponsive. I experienced this myself on a few occasions but . . . but Max had seemed so *into* it.

"Did I—do something?" My voice sounds pitifully small, far off, as if emanating from someone else across the room. A loathsome, oily sense of shame rises in my throat as my mind flashes to Elliot without warning.

"No, no," Max says with a chuckle, placing his palms on my knees. "Hand to God. I would like nothing more than to lay you down and give you everything we *both* want—I'm sorry I'm not able to at the moment." His tone is genuine. Despite my confusion, I start to believe him.

"Oh—well, I completely understand. Don't worry about it."

I sit up and cross my legs, forcing a smile as I pull a pillow under my arms lengthwise to cover my body. Max shifts beside me, reclining on his back with one arm folded beneath his head, the entirety of him still on full display.

"Listen, I used to party really fucking hard. Years and years of it," he begins, the fingers of his free hand tracing small patterns over my knee. "I was on a mad one—wouldn't change it if I could," he laughs, his eyes far off. "But sadly, I've paid the price of a good time now. Can't always rise to the occasion when the situation calls for it." He shrugs, meeting my gaze.

I seem to have succumbed to an age-old feminine instinct— that urge to either assume responsibility or comfort him, fearing somewhere deep down that if I don't, his humiliation will sour into something darker. Max's smile and relaxed demeanor are disarming, a stark contrast to the encounters I had previously when this particular issue arose—or rather, didn't.

"I really do understand," I reply finally. "I'm just glad it isn't me."

"How you could even think that is beyond me," he laughs sincerely in return. "You're unbelievably sexy—every move, every sound. Trust and believe—no man would ever see the sight I just saw and disagree."

"Thank you." I smile sadly. "My ex—" I swallow hard as I prepare to say the name I haven't dared utter in months for the second time tonight. "Elliot and I struggled with chemistry. I always felt it but was too scared to say anything. I loved him and just wanted things to work. In the end, when there was nothing left to lose, he admitted that he found me *aesthetically* attractive, that he liked having me on his arm, but he'd never really found me . . . sexually desirable."

The words sting my tongue as the memory flashes somewhere behind my eyes. The countless nights I reached for Elliot, only to be shrugged away with excuses of fatigue and early mornings. It was hard not to conclude that this was the reason for everything that followed—that I simply wasn't enough to hold his attention.

Max furrows his brow as he listens. I expect him to interject with another boilerplate dismissal of my attraction to "fools," but instead, he asks quietly, "Did you find him sexually desirable?"

"I think at first. It's hard to remember now, but in retrospect . . . we never seemed to fit together right."

"Too small?" He flashes a cheeky grin, raising his hips slightly as he stretches—an unsubtle display of what isn't small.

"Nothing like *that*." I shoot him a look. "It just always felt like he was running a playbook he'd used a hundred times before without really engaging with *me*." I pause, considering my words for a moment as I look off into the past. "I really get off on being . . . watched and enjoyed. I like when I can *see* the lust in the other person's eyes. Feel how badly they want me." I shake my head.

Looking over at Max, I see that his thoughtful expression has returned, the gears of his mind whirring just beneath the surface, though I can't be sure what he's thinking exactly. I can't be sure what I'm thinking exactly either, revealing parts of myself I don't share with anyone.

"My ex-fiancée was beautiful—very alluring, very seductive," he begins, running a hand through his hair. "When we first started out, she really put on a show, but over time, I realized that's all it was—a performance." His eyes remain far off, roving over something I can't see. "She wanted to be desired by everyone, and most people she encountered obliged. I really didn't mind at first—I was secure enough, and I loved being with the girl everyone wanted." He shrugs, a shadow moving behind his eyes. "But she loved toying with me most of all—she wanted to feel how much I wanted her while reminding me that she could slip away at any moment."

He appears lost in memory. I settle into a new awareness—the presence of two other people in this house now, the ghosts of our pasts.

"That's not what I meant when I said I like to be watched."

"I know." He smiles warmly at me. "If anything, I imagine we felt similarly in our last relationships. Decorative and even useful at times, but not really desired. Not really wanted or appreciated fully."

I nod. The still-wounded part of my heart aches at his words—at the sound of my truth on his lips.

"Now," Max says, his tone newly animated as he rolls onto his side to face me. "I do want to acknowledge what a *tremendous* turning point we've just reached." I watch him in bewilderment as he continues. "When I asked back there on our walk what gets you off in the bedroom, I thought you'd eat the head off me. Now you've gone and told me of your own volition." He clicks his tongue, and I roll my eyes.

"*That's* the turning point? Not you having your fingers inside me a few minutes ago?"

He pretends to ponder the question for a moment. "Yeah, I'd have to say so. You said you wouldn't tell me because we were strangers, so I take this to mean we're properly acquainted now."

74

"Hardly," I snort.

"Hardly strangers or hardly acquainted?"

"I don't know—both. In a way, I feel like we met ten minutes ago, and in another, I feel like we've known each other for ten years."

A slow smile spreads over Max's face again. "I know what you mean."

Our eyes meet, and a comfortable silence passes between us. I wonder if this is where I should suggest my departure. No part of me wants to get up, redress, and find the words to say goodbye, but if sex, the driving force behind this late-night visit, is off the table—I don't have much reason to stay, do I?

"You know," Max sits up suddenly, positioning himself in front of me, "just because I can't fuck you right now doesn't mean we can't still have some fun."

"Oh?" I tease, quietly elated.

In one smooth motion, he grabs both of my ankles, eliciting a squeal from me as he pulls, dragging me down the bed until I lie flat-backed, still grasping the pillow. Gently, he removes my goose-down shield, positioning himself between my legs as he leans in, pressing his soft lips against my mouth. His slow, sensual kisses trail down my jaw and along my neck, over the valley of my collarbones and the peak of my nipple. I prop myself up to watch, my skin prickling as he carries on along my sternum and down my stomach, again stopping just below my navel as his eyes lift to meet mine. I exhale deeply—my answer to his silent request for permission given as I lie back in waiting.

Eyes closed, I feel the velvet expanse of Max's lips brush against my inner thigh and brace myself as he moves inward, the warmth of his breath alerting me to his location. His tongue moves slowly at first, an exploration—pressured and deliberate but teasing once again. The syncopated rhythm of it keeps me on edge, every stroke like a current jolting down my limbs to the tips of my toes and fingers. He lifts his head for a moment, and I raise myself up slightly, a flash of panic and confusion rushing through me as he laughs softly.

"Don't worry, I'm not done."

My pulse jumps when he pulls me closer, thumbs kneading the sensitive hollows of my pelvis where hips meet torso. One finger enters slowly, then two—I melt away as his mouth and tongue find me again, moving with a still maddeningly light touch. I writhe against his fingers, angling for more of everything as he hums his exhale, driving deeper and deeper. Heat pulsates through me as the curling of his fingers brings about a mounting pressure low in my stomach.

Not yet, I think as I try to steady my ragged breathing. I've been known to take ages, always requiring a surgical focus to get myself there, but this is different. I'm under Max's control, reactive to his every move. His entire essence is seductive. The hunger in his eyes, the need when he forgets himself and becomes the pure embodiment of desire—a voyeur, lost in observation rather than performance. I don't know if he understands my exhibitionism and has chosen to play the part or if we just . . . *fit*.

The sensation of suction interrupts my thoughts, and I let out an involuntary gasp, the muscles of my abdomen tensing. Shimmering waves of warmth pass over me as he brings me higher and higher, closer and closer. I twist beneath him, my fingers raking over the bedsheets as his unoccupied hand grasps my bucking hip, and he uses his full strength to restrain me. The thought of his power over me is intoxicating—I contemplate testing the boundaries to see just how firm he can be, but I can't risk disrupting his technique.

My mind wanders wildly as I try to stave off my impending climax, but I have no control. The feeling cuts through everything, permeating every level of my being and tethering me to the present moment. To the pressure of his strong hand and the warm caress of his tongue, his beckoning fingers, and the draw of his mouth against me.

Surrendering at last, the wave of building pleasure crests with blinding heat before it falls, the rolling aftershocks moving through me as residual bursts of electricity. I lie there, unable to move or speak for what feels like eons as Max sprawls out beside me.

"Thanks," I say finally once I catch my breath. I want to laugh imagining myself from a birds-eye view on this strange bed, beneath the roof of this strange house beside this strange man—how far I've come from just this morning.

"My pleasure," Max chuckles as I flip over onto my stomach.

"Can I ask you something?"

Max turns to look at me as I reach out, my fingers moving over the tattoo on his chest. "Who's Catríona?"

He looks puzzled before glancing down his nose as if he's forgotten the name emblazoned in ink is there. "Oh yeah—pronounced *Cat-ree-na*," he corrects gently. "My mother."

"Is she . . ."

"Alive and well." He smiles, but there's something pained behind his eyes.

"Are you two close?"

"I haven't seen her in a while, but we chat on the phone often. It's a bit complicated—"

"You don't have to share, I'm sorry," I interrupt.

"Don't be," he says, flashing a small reassuring smile. "My parents don't exactly have a perfect marriage. My father is a brilliant man, but he's also quite cruel." The reflection of warm lamplight glows in his dark eyes as he looks off into the past. "He's flaunted numerous affairs in front of my mother. And he's never been physically abusive as far as I know, but he's screamed at her from morning till night for as long as I can remember."

"I'm so sorry," I murmur, a pain thrumming somewhere deep within at the thought of it all, at his mother's torment and a little Max witnessing it.

"It is what it is." He sighs, looking toward the ceiling. "My sister Siobhan and I have tried many times over the years to get my mother out from under my father's thumb, but every time she comes close, it's like he can sense it. He starts acting right, swears off the other women, buys her flowers, speaks kindly to her, all that." He turns to meet my gaze. "Siobhan takes it very personally when our mam stays, but I'm easy on her—it's hard getting out from under something like that."

I nod, brushing my fingers absently over the soft green fabric beneath me. "I'm sure that when you've been made to feel small for that long, it's hard to feel like you deserve anything else."

Max nods sadly. "Don't get me wrong, she's a very strong woman—my sister and I were up the walls as kids, and she managed us just fine without killing our spirits. She is blindly devoted to my father, but I've never looked at her as being weak." He raises his eyebrows. "If anything, she's the picture of restraint—she could've easily poisoned him years ago."

"Saint Catríona the Patient." Max laughs wholeheartedly at this. I watch as his levity flickers back into pain before he returns to the room.

"So, on another note," he begins, sitting up, "I don't want to be presumptuous, but I'm sure it's quite late now, and I would hope that you decided to stay the night."

I have not decided, actually—as I turn to look at him, I realize the thought barely entered my mind at all. I regard sleeping beside someone to be one of the most intimate acts, and the idea of doing so is more daunting than ever. It's been so long since I shared a bed with someone other than Lexi. Since I slept and breathed and turned and dreamed beside a man—who isn't Elliot.

Somehow, I sense that waking up beside Max will mean I can no longer languish in heartbreak purgatory—the wasteland of the in-between. It will mark some new phase of acceptance—letting go and inviting those "endless possibilities." With just a few words, I can move forward.

"Yeah," I reply. "I'll stay."

VIII

Sleep. It's been a struggle over the past year. Not only the glaring absence of a person beside me—one who will never return to my bed—but also the nightmares that came afterward as the dust settled. They were always the same: my hand on a doorknob, turning slowly as a cry I knew to be my own echoed around the room, urging me not to open the door. Not to reveal the scene behind it that would remain etched into my mind.

But something shifted in the last few months—I was able to sleep through the night and well into the morning. Now I sleep all the time—though I often debate whether this new habit is the flip side of the same depression coin or the turn of a newer, healthier leaf.

As I look at Max, I worry that his presence might disturb the peace I only just found, but I decide he doesn't need to know all of that. For what feels like the first time in hours, I don't reveal myself to him completely. I simply warn him that I have "sleep issues."

"Well, in that case, I'll make you as comfortable as I possibly can," Max says as he rises and dons his underwear. "For starters, would you like something to wear?"

I nod, and he crosses to the wide wooden dresser on the far wall. Rifling around, he withdraws a faded band tee, holding it up for me to see.

"Will Thin Lizzy bring you comfort?"

I laugh softly. "Absolutely."

"These too—no sense in disturbing the evidence of your strip tease back there in the living room." He tosses me the shirt along with a pair of gray boxer briefs. "Now—what would you say to me bringing that bottle of vodka in here for some more getting to know each other?"

I don't want to know what time it is, but I don't have the willpower to stop myself from glancing at the clock glowing from the bedside table: 1:24 a.m.—could be worse. Having settled on where I'm sleeping, it doesn't really matter anyway. There will be no anxious moment crossing the threshold of my apartment to face an empty house in a quiet world. No, by the time I return home, the sun will be high and bright—I can make phone calls and pick up coffee from a café. I won't have to face whatever transpired this evening alone.

"I'm not tired—bring it on," I reply as I pull on the tee and settle into a cross-legged position.

Max returns a few minutes later, the bottle of Grey Goose, two ice-filled glasses, and a tall Mountain Valley water balanced precariously in his arms.

"Sadly, as this *is* a bachelor pad, I don't have anything in the way of fizzy drinks at the moment. Figured we'd drink it on the rocks, put some hair on our chests, and if you need a chaser"—he holds up the deep green vessel like a bottle girl at a club—"I've got some delicious, refreshing still water."

"Fantastic." I grimace, my stomach turning at the thought of straight alcohol.

Max fiddles with his phone until Leonard Cohen's "Dance Me to the End of Love" fills the room. When he's satisfied with the volume, he pours our respective cups of poison, handing me one as he sits on the edge of the bed.

"To—"

"To even *more* endless possibilities," I interrupt, clinking his glass before he has a chance to react. "Good choice on the music."

He lights up excitedly. "This record, in particular, was really inspiring to me growing up. That *rasp* and raw power behind his poetry—it made me want to be a musician too." He takes a drink, moving to settle his back against the pillows. "We also share a birthday."

"And when's that?"

Max pauses, squinting with mock suspicion. "I know you women and your witchcraft." He raises a pointed finger. "Go on, ask me."

"Ask you what?" I laugh in genuine confusion.

"*You* want to give me an astrological once-over, and lucky for you"—he lifts his finger, eyebrows raised as his expression softens—"I happen to know all three of my signs."

The burning liquid shoots down my windpipe as I choke on my drink, spluttering and coughing, fighting for air through my laughter. Max hands me the bottle of water, and I drink gratefully.

"Please," I wheeze. "Do tell."

"I'm a Virgo," he begins with comedic cheer. "My rising sign is Aries, and my other one—"

"Moon sign."

"Yeah, moon—that's Pisces."

"And what does that combination say about you?"

Max looks at me, aghast. "Well, I haven't a clue—I only just got to Los Angeles. That's meant to be *your* department."

"I'm not that well-versed in the astrological arts!" I laugh. "My friend Lexi, on the other hand, does *all* of that—she could tell you."

"I know," Max says, his eyes glowing mirthfully. "How'd you think I learned my 'big three'?" He draws dramatic air quotes as the memory of him seated and laughing with my friends at Bar Sperl returns to me.

"Ahh—"

"They're good people, your friends." He smiles kindly. "That Lexi—very *loud*, first of all." I laugh quietly as he continues. "But she loves you."

"She's family," I say with a thoughtful smile. "Met when we were four years old and have pretty much been inseparable ever since."

"And what do you love about her?"

Another meat-and-potatoes question. Simple, inelegant, and yet, somehow—substantive beyond measure.

"I couldn't possibly tell you every reason." I shake my head. "But for one, I love her stubbornness—she won't budge on an opinion until she really, truly understands why she should change her mind. You'll never catch her agreeing for the sake of agreement. She's one of the most *real* and honest people I've ever met."

I pause, a question dawning on me. "Wait, what about your bandmates?"

A blank expression crosses Max's face as he takes a long drink. "What about them?"

"When did you meet? What are their names? Are you close? You haven't told me anything about them."

"Are we back to the question game?" he asks. "Because that's three right there."

I give him an unamused look as he adjusts his position and says, "Fine. There's not much to tell. Conor's on drums, James plays guitar, and on bass—" Another drink as he pauses. "Sean. We all met in secondary school, got into playing together at some point, and kicked off the band seriously when I was twenty-four." He rubs his muscled shoulder with his free hand. "We were thick as thieves once, but we've been together now through lengthy tours, industry people, artistic disputes, messy relationships, and all that." He looks up, smiling ruefully. "It's not like it was when we were just a bunch of lads who wanted to make music."

I ignore my curiosity over the emphasis on his bassist's name and simply nod, indicating with the forward motion of my glass that it's his turn to ask. Max studies my face for a moment.

"What made you want to be a writer?"

"I guess poetry was the gateway drug. We learned about the classics in high school—Langston Hughes, Maya Angelou, Emily Dickinson, Walt Whitman. I'd started writing all this intense stuff trying to imitate them, but it didn't really *fit* right—I hadn't found my voice." I absently stroke the length of a single braid as I speak. "I remember one day, my mom gave me this collection of beatnik poetry, and I happened to open it up to 'Howl' by Allen Ginsberg." I pause, raising my eyebrows for dramatic effect. "Imagine my surprise after having only read these beautiful, traditional poets

when I saw the words 'cock' and 'balls' right there on the page."
Max laughs heartily as I continue. "It was . . . exciting to me.
Not because I wanted to write anything like that necessarily, but
because I didn't know that you could defy tradition like that and
be accepted—or even celebrated for it."

"The revolution began with cock and balls," Max says in a
theatrical voice.

I laugh. "Hey, like I said, we can't control what inspires us. I
know it sounds funny, but that was the moment I realized every
artist can make their own rules. I think that's what my mother
was trying to show me."

"She sounds like a very wise woman," he says sincerely.

I nod, tipping my glass in a silent toast to her. "A crafty one
too. Always wanted me to tell stories of some kind, so she filled
my head with myths, legends, poems, and prose from all over the
world until I didn't have a choice. I had to write." I smile. "My
father's always been the practical one—he wanted me to focus
on something that people do to make money in the 'real world.'"

"As someone with an entirely made-up job that's paid fairly
well over the years, I can't say I agree with your father there.
Sometimes, the more we live in fantasy, the better off we're
rewarded." Max downs the rest of his drink and grabs the bottle.
"Your parents sound like they're worlds apart."

"They couldn't be more opposite. When they met in the early
nineties, she was an acupuncturist specializing in energy healing
and Chinese medicine. He was a divorce lawyer." I let out a sharp
exhale, shaking my head. "Listen, I'm glad to be here—but how
they got together will always be a total mystery to me. I think the
only thing they ever really agreed on was their separation." I pause,

recalling the hazy memory of my parents' brief romantic union as Max tops up my drink. "You know, they say your parents model relationships for you—and unfortunately, I think by watching them, I learned how to overcompromise. How to abandon who you are in order to make things work."

He smiles sadly. "I hear you."

I try to sip casually, but my throat is raw, and I can't help my sour face. "So," I ask, "what's your favorite Dog from Hell song?"

He rolls his eyes exaggeratedly, and I uncross my legs to nudge him with my foot, but he catches me by the ankle, looking into my eyes as he holds me hostage. Instead of retaliation, he runs his hand up my calf, slowly and sensually, the warmth and strength of his touch eliciting another electric pulse.

"I've been working on a new one actually—it's called 'Oenone,'" he replies, his fingertips working their way up my shin. "It's about the Greek mythological nymph who married Paris of Troy. He left her for Helen, who was said to be the most beautiful woman in the world, but his choice started the Trojan War." He reaches my knee and gives a little squeeze, triggering my patellar reflex as he recites, "*The only mourner come to cry, he gave away and chose to die, and aft she wept and said farewell, he'd on the pyre and straight to hell.*"

"That's very beautiful—and sad," I murmur.

"I've always loved Greek mythology—the gods are just as messed up as the mortals, capable of jealousy, hope, wrath—love." He swirls the waning ice cubes in his glass. "Just learning lessons and paying for their sins like everyone else."

"Was there an Oenone in your life?"

The question leaves my lips without thought. The motion of his hand on my leg falters as his eyes flick upward to meet mine.

"Grace," he replies after a moment. "I didn't leave her outright, but I might as well have. We met just as the band was starting—she was with me through the whole beginning, all the ups and downs, every bit of it." He sighs. "Three years in, the band started to reach some success, and it wasn't long after that she noticed I was slipping toward darkness—choosing partying and fame over everything that really mattered. I was so fucking *arrogant*." He shakes his head as if still in disbelief after all this time. "I was young, women wanted me, and my star was on the rise, so when she asked me to slow down, I told her that was just how it was going to be." He closes his eyes, wincing at the sight of his past. "She was gone before I even had a chance to sober up and realize what I'd lost."

"Where is she now?"

"Married. Living in Lisbon." Max's smile has a hint of sadness. "We've spoken just once since—she's got two baby girls, and she's very happy." He rubs his eyes. "Even if I'd listened to her, I don't think we would've worked. I would've wasted her regardless, either by my hedonism or just the grind of life on the road back then. I'm glad she's got everything she always dreamed of now."

More ghosts, I think. I can feel them all around us.

"And who was your Helen of Troy?"

Max chuckles darkly as he busies himself smoothing faint wrinkles on the duvet. "It was years after Grace, and I still hadn't slowed down, not by a long shot. We were starting out our US tour with a show at Webster Hall in New York, and the opener was this pretty American girl—Lilah Dane."

Lilah Dane—now that's a name I know. It somehow burned its way into my brain as I rode in Emily's car the one time I was permitted to third-wheel her and Lexi's big night out. Emily put on Lilah's music, gushing excitedly that she was "everything" and "the moment," but after just a few bars, Lexi very matter-of-factly declared that she wasn't a fan. I secretly took pleasure in watching Emily's profile go crestfallen from the backseat.

"Lilah was the embodiment of my darkest fantasies at that time. She was sexy, mysterious, and even more hungry for fame and fortune than I was—but she loved games. She asked me daily, hourly, to pledge my love for her, then bragged about all the men around us, my peers and friends who wanted to fuck her and how easy it would be to have her pick." He scrubs a hand over his face as if even the memory tires him. "She'd go on the lash for days, out with god-knows-who doing god-knows-what, then told me I was trying to control her when I asked where she'd been." He swallows hard. "She ridiculed me in public, picking fights in front of everyone—then swore to change in private."

"Why didn't you *leave*?" Again, the question rushes out before I consider it. Max raises his eyes, weighty now with sadness, to find my own.

"It's what I was taught."

His words hang in the air between us, and my skin prickles with a phantom chill. The album ends, the poignant lyrics of the final song swirling all around us as I reach toward him, my fingers brushing his cheek and lingering there. As if on instinct, he places his hand over mine, running his lips over my palm as he meets my gaze. My pulse quickens at the reflexive gesture—the strange intimacy of it. At this moment, at least, there seems to be no question whether or not we've known each other for eons.

"I understand," I say tenderly as he releases my hand.

"I know."

Max sits up, retrieving his glass as he moves beside me, lying back against the pillows again.

"Any musical requests?" he asks, grabbing his phone from the nightstand. "And *don't* say Dog from Hell—listen on your own time."

"Fine." I consider. "Play . . . 'Astral Weeks.'"

"Van Morrison?" Max asks, and I read the intrigue on his face. "Interesting."

"I just picked him because my first choice of Irish musicians wasn't an option," I mock. Max smirks as he fulfills my request, and the first notes of a familiar melody find my ears.

My mind still swirls with questions as we drink in the music, Max with his eyes closed, humming along softly as he thumps his chest in a syncopated rhythm.

"When did you and Lilah break up?" I ask, emboldened by the effects of the vodka.

Max's eyes remain closed, and a hardness flickers over his face. "Nearly two years ago now."

His resistance is obvious. I hesitate as a sense of social decorum attempts to permeate my haze. A strange feeling gnaws at my gut.

There's something hidden here, comes the warning, a whisper from deep within my mind.

Ask him.

"How did it end?"

I watch the twitch of Max's brow. Several beats pass before he says a word. "She left."

His eyes blink open as he turns his head and sees the earnest look on my face. I watch his gaze move to my lips as a strange, sad smile plays over his mouth.

Ask him, my inner voice hisses again.

But I don't have to.

"We stayed in contact long distance for about six months after first meeting on tour, but eventually, I moved to New York to be with her," he begins. "I proposed quickly in the heat of it all, but the honeymoon phase ended almost immediately. In a matter of months, it was hell. We'd fight, I'd apologize to keep peace, and we'd drink and fuck to forget." I watch his hands, which are still folded over his chest, but his thumbs drum in an anxious, jumpy rhythm. "She was hitting it hard, but I couldn't hack it anymore. My body couldn't take the endless nights and horrible, wasted days."

His throat bobs as he pauses for a long moment, something like nervousness flooding through him. I sense my own uptick of anxiety, like the sharp jumping needle of a polygraph test, though I can't quite understand why.

"I felt lost—I still loved her and couldn't let go of the good times." His eyes plead as they bore into mine. "She could be so thoughtful and loving when she wanted to be. I didn't want to face the reality that we didn't belong together, that it was totally fucked." He inhales deeply, steadying himself as he continues more carefully, "I think she'd started to hate me—I think she felt I was weak for not just walking away and wanted to see how far she could push me." Another hard swallow, like he's forcing down stones. "I didn't plan for it, but maybe somewhere deep down, I knew I wouldn't leave unless it was broken beyond repair. It only ever happened the one time—"

A shiver runs through me, my breath quickens, and that icy voice cuts through my mind once more.

Danger.

Not again.

My mouth runs dry as the end of the story unfolds in front of me. The music is ill-fitting now—the sound of jaunty trumpets and sunny drumbeats ringing in my ears like keening sirens. I hear my own words, muted and muffled as if I'm underwater. Not a question—but a declaration of what I already know.

"You cheated. That's it. You're a cheater."

IX

Max's face is muddled with emotions. Some are indecipherable, but others, like surprise, hurt, and guilt, are easy to read. Heat radiates through my skull as I become a passenger beside the mounting panic, grabbing for the wheel, angling for control of the car.

"It was a mistake," he starts, his brow furrowed with both defensiveness and confusion. "I was drunk and lonely. It was a girl who—"

"*That's* the line you're going with?" I spit the words. "You think you're the first person to blame it on alcohol and *loneliness*? Every cheater claims that it just happened, that it was a mistake, and they'll pay every day for the rest of their lives—"

"I *have* paid. I will *continue* to pay." His tone is sharp but measured. "I was miserable and cowardly, I can accept that, but I won't accept the identity of a 'cheater'—like I'm irredeemable. She was pushing me away every single day—"

I snap. "You had every right to leave, but instead, you decided to take the easy way out."

"It wasn't the fucking easy way—Shera, are you insane?" Max

realizes his poor word choice almost instantaneously. I stare fire into his eyes.

"I am insane, actually. I came home with a complete fucking *stranger* and somehow deluded myself into believing it was a good idea—"

"So that's it? One mistake from my past is enough to write me off completely?"

I don't answer. I only look over his handsome face, disheveled hair, and muscled chest, heaving beneath the weight of his breath, and think to myself, *What a waste.* What a waste of trust and hope. Max isn't the man I believed him to be. Not the playboy with a heart of gold. Not the spell-breaker sent to awaken some long-dormant part of me. He's not his mother's child; he's his father's son. He's selfish, a coward—predictably weak in his attempted portrayal of victimhood. He conned me, fooled me, *betrayed* me.

"Hey." His voice is calm as he inches forward, moving his hand to my knee. My skin prickles, but I don't recoil. "Look, I—I don't understand this, any of this." He waves a hand vaguely over the bitter air between us. "But I want you to understand *me*—it was a moment of weakness, the biggest moment of weakness I've ever had in my life . . ."

His voice becomes distant as that familiar panic rises up like bile in my throat and a high, tinny ringing fills my ears. My breaths turn shallow as every inhale drags through my lungs, faster and faster, the edges of my vision blurring.

This is my doing. Something within me now always seeks out the cracks. Something within me is determined to prove that no one can truly be trusted.

"Shera—slow down." Max's voice is a buzzy hum reverberating through my body.

An hour ago, I was at the threshold of mounting climax, and now I'm on the precipice of a panic attack. Max's voice continues in the background, imploring me—but it's too late. I begin to hyperventilate, spasms of breath ripping through my chest as his hand becomes my only tether to the room around me.

This can't be real—I can't be breaking down so fully, so completely. Not when I've carefully stitched my seams together over months and months, reinforcing them daily, testing their sturdiness against painful memories of happy times, against sideways glances and saccharine pity. And yet here I am. Ripped to shreds by a memory that doesn't even belong to me. In the company of a man I met only a few hours ago.

"Feel my hands on your shoulders, feel the weight of them." Max's voice reaches me again, a soft tendril attempting to draw me back to him as my breath continues in jumping spurts. "Look at me," he says, but I avoid his gaze. "*Look* at me." His hands are on my face now, pulling me gently until I have no choice but to do as he asks.

As our eyes meet, the levee within me breaks. Tears roll down my face, as if from some bottomless well of despair. I can't help but notice the depths behind Max's eyes as they stare back—the worry, not only for my anger toward him but also for the wounded parts of me that are now so clearly visible.

"C'mere." He moves over the bed, taking my hands as he steps to the floor. "Stand up." I feel him hauling me to my feet now as I lose contact with my limbs, his strong arms supporting me while my wild breath brings me higher.

We cross the room, and his voice continues urging calm with gently soothing words I can't quite make out. As we enter the bathroom, I feel the changes of flooring beneath my feet—the rough kilim rug becoming smooth wood grain, then giving way to cool, hard concrete.

Max guides me to sit on the toilet's closed lid before stepping away to turn the handles of the large walk-in shower. Water bursts from the two heads on opposite walls as he returns to my side, running his hands over my arms while observing my fragile state, still gasping for air. Slowly, carefully, he lifts the hem of my borrowed T-shirt, pulling it over my head as the humidity meets my bare skin. Again, he helps me stand, removing my boxer briefs next, abandoning the sensuality of our previous disrobing in favor of simple, focused care.

"Maybe this isn't pressing at the moment—and I hope to god I'm not making a mistake in even touching them—but I don't want the water to mess up your pretty hair and risk you raging at me about it later," Max says as he awkwardly gathers my braids, piling them messily into a bun on top of my head. His hands are tentative and tender—when he finishes, he stares for a moment as if unsure what to do next before using an errant strand to wrap and fasten his handiwork. After testing its sturdiness with a small nudge, he gently guides me toward the flowing water.

As the steam envelops me, I feel the heat draw the panic from me bit by bit, encouraging my breathing to slow. Absent the oxygen deprivation, my tears slow too, and small, stuttering inhalations shudder through my body like aftershocks as the water rains over me. Suddenly, I feel the pressure of Max's hands on my shoulders.

"Feeling better?"

I nod mutely, focusing on the white subway tiles before me.

"I used to have panic attacks." His fingers move over my shoulders, gingerly kneading the muscle. "Cold helps too, but I figured a hot shower would be preferred." I say nothing, and his hands slow. A few moments pass before he implores, "Please look at me."

As I turn, I see that he kept on his underwear, now water-logged. He stands close, his muscled chest nearly brushing against my exposed breasts, but he doesn't so much as glance downward.

"I know you have a low opinion of me right now—I won't pretend to know why this has affected you so much, and I won't try to defend myself." He pauses, drawing a hand down his face as he wipes away the droplets beading on his forehead. "But if you'll listen, I'd like to tell you the rest of the story."

I study his face—his soft lips slicked with moisture, the wet locks of his brown hair now sticking to his knitted brow. I'm a stranger, standing naked before him after melting down into a molten mass of sharp, unyielding steel. And yet—here he is. I suppose it's an even exchange. I can listen—I will listen.

"Tell me," I say quietly, the sound of falling water echoing around us. Max inhales deeply.

"We fought the night it happened," he begins. "We were out at a bar with the band—everyone was in town to work on our new album, and to no one's surprise, Lilah had been on the tear even before we arrived." His throat bobs as he looks away. "She was a master at pushing my buttons, and she knew I had one particularly large, bright-red blinking one in the shape of our bassist, Sean. He and I had a . . . bit of a history with women.

It was easy for her to play into my paranoias." Max leans his elbow against the shower wall and rakes his fingers through his hair. "Lilah was getting pretty friendly with him as the night went on—she was always flirtatious, but something felt different. At some point, I got up for the jacks and found them in the hallway—she was pressed against him, whispering in his ear. He had his hands on her waist." He licks his lips, shaking his head as his eyes return to me. "I flew off the handle—I just felt so disrespected, even though deep down I only had myself to blame for not walking away ages earlier. Sean went all smug and quiet, but she gave as good as she got. Told me every vile, hateful thing she thought about me—two fucking years' worth of it."

The heat of the shower feels oppressive, but I don't dare disturb the sanctity of this strange confessional. Priest and penitent, enclosed within the tiled walls. I want—no, I *need* to understand Lilah—to empathize with whatever pain drove her to cruelty. She didn't deserve betrayal, but . . . listening to Max's story, it's hard not to imagine the desperation he must have reached. The low that brought him even lower.

"We had some words, then I left. Went to another pub down the road and tried to drink myself out of it." He sighs, wiping at his face again as the steam hangs thick in the air around us. "I was hammered by the time she walked in—this girl." Max swallows, and I stiffen almost imperceptibly. "She was . . . a fan. I wanted to feel adored, to feel special. She invited me back to hers, and we—"

"Not this part," I murmur, placing a hand against his firm chest. He nods, his eyes dropping to the floor. "What happened after?" I ask. "How did she find out?"

"I told her." His voice is quiet, low and heavy. "I got home around four a.m.—she was still up, still out of her head. I felt sober as a judge by then—the weight of what I'd done just cut right through it all."

"What did she do—when you told her?" My words crackle out in a hoarse whisper.

Max huffs ruefully as he shakes his head. "I saw the shock on her face—the hurt. I braced myself for punishment—I *wanted* punishment, but instead, it was just these silent tears. I tried to touch her, to comfort her in some way, but she pulled away and just said, 'I didn't think you had it in you.'"

My stomach turns. I feel it through the ether—the icy cold that must have run through her at Max's disclosure. The choice she made to hold her composure. Maybe I can't fully relate to Lilah—her urge for chaos and provocation—but I can see my reflection clear as day in the image of her heart breaking.

"She left the house that morning and didn't come back for days. Conor was the one who told me she'd gone to Sean's. I've been told that was the first time—that I drove them to do exactly what I'd accused them of." He pinches the bridge of his nose as he breathes out a steadying exhale. "I told you that I paid for it and that I'll continue to pay—that wasn't a line. Our relationship was already cobbled together with fucking nails and glue, but I broke something irreparable that night, and Lilah wasn't the only person I lost."

"Well, you may have betrayed her, but Sean—he's your friend. He betrayed you."

Max shakes his head. "Sean and I have always had tension—he's hot-headed. I can be too. There's an undercurrent of competition." He looks away as he gathers his next words. "Truth is, we both had our eyes on Grace at the start, but she picked me. Later, when she was in a state about my bad habits, Sean was in my ear telling me that she was dead weight and I was better off without her." A long pause as he continues to gaze off into another world. "One night years after, when he was off his face, he told me that he'd never stopped loving her. He'd resented me for how I treated her and knew she'd be better off if I set her free."

My gauge for empathy spins as wildly as the needle of a compass. Such flawed people—all of them. Driven by desire, by need, by pain, by love. Maybe there are no perfect monsters—no absolute villains. Maybe every evil deed can be traced back to a break that changed someone's perception of the entire world—the moment they felt cheated and decided not to play the game with honor.

"How are you and Sean now after—"

"I was feeling so low after everything, I think I directed all the anger I felt toward myself at him. Once we hashed it all out, there was just so much to deal with—years of resentments on both sides—but I've forgiven him now. And said my apologies too." He shrugs. "We'll never be the way we were again, but we can come together over the music and get the job done."

I nod. I can feel the baby hairs around my face curling in the moisture. Looking down, my hands are so puckered and pruned that my fingertips turned pale.

"I want to get out," I say. Max searches my face. He nods, and I turn the shower handle, my skin pulsating as I adjust to the absence of streaming water.

I stand dripping as he fetches two fresh white towels from the linen closet and holds one out to me. As he removes his now-sopping underwear and I busy myself with drying, I steal a glance at his naked form, muscles glistening in the warm light. He is rather beautiful—so beautiful that if I think too much about it, I know the tears will return in an instant. This is probably the last time I'll ever see Max King.

Stepping back into the bedroom, Max slips into fresh under-wear and takes a seat on the bed while I wrap and tuck the towel around myself. I reach up and undo the topknot he secured, shaking out my braids as they fall around my shoulders.

"Did I make the right move with that?" He gestures toward my hair, now wavy from its bun and our lengthy shower.

"You did." I give him a half smile. "It would've been dripping wet for hours otherwise."

He exhales relief, nodding as he leans forward, bracing his elbows on his knees. I watch as he tiredly scrubs his hands over his face.

"I need to go home," I declare suddenly.

Max freezes midmotion. He looks at me. "Shera, it's nearly three—"

"I listened like you asked, but I can't stay."

Max's eyes narrow, his keen puzzlement lined with concern as he says, "I know you think you don't know me—right now especially—but this evening, I've bared more of myself to you than I have to anyone. In a very long time." His face is earnest. "I feel I can trust you, and I swear you can trust me."

A lump forms in my throat. Everything that's only just quieted within me begins to churn again.

"I just need to go," I whisper.

"Please—don't leave." He brings his palms together, hands in prayer. "Please, I—I'm actually begging." He rises and steps toward me. "I don't want to leave things a mess."

I recoil. "It's my fault—I'm clearly not ready for this." I shake my head. "Whatever the fuck *this* is."

Something like hurt crosses Max's face. He studies me. "Tell me, why was my story so personal to you?"

No—not that.

I already crumbled in front of him, already soured something easy and carefree. I can't bear to reveal the rest—the deeply rooted seed of all that misplaced anguish. There's still a way out now—even after everything that's transpired, I can still make an excuse. I can text him tomorrow, apologize for my meltdown, and blame it on the wine, the vodka, the moon, *anything*. We'll exchange a few pleasant messages making light of it all before mutually deciding to stop. He'll be a fond memory, and I'll be a crazy story.

"It doesn't matter. I shouldn't have come here—I'm sorry for all of this, I really am—"

"That's a load of bollocks!" he exclaims. "Everything was going fine—"

"It wasn't fine." The cold detachment of my voice sounds foreign even to my ears, and Max's face falls. "It was *never* fine. I don't think you're irredeemable, but what you did—you don't understand. Once you've done that, once you've broken that moral code—"

"Is *that* what it's all about?" He scoffs. "Your own personal sense of *piety*? Like you've never done anything to hurt someone, *Saint Shera*?" His tone is vindictive now.

"Of course I have," I snap, anger boiling. "But I've never followed my dick and ruined someone's life in the process."

"I told you that I paid the price—you think I'd ever blow up my life like that again?"

I laugh cruelly. "If the right fan walked into the right bar—"

"Shera, it meant *nothing*!"

"*Nothing*?" I hiss, the fire flaring again as my insides churn. No panic, no disassociation now—I'm in my body fully, coiled like a snake, my tail rattling as I warn of my impending strike.

"Maybe for you—but it's *everything* to me."

X

The silence is deafening, interrupted only by the droning of a car engine in the far distance. Max squints as if trying to determine whether or not he misheard me. I take a step toward where he stands, still blocking the narrow walkway between the bed and dresser.

"Please move," I say, avoiding eye contact. When he doesn't budge, I repeat myself, this time looking him full in the face. "Please. Move. *Now.*"

The heat of his searching, knowing gaze is too much to bear. I feel him slacken with realization. I push past him, and he finally obliges, stepping out of my way as our bodies brush against each other.

I speed through the narrow hallway and out into the open living room, scanning the floor around the sofa for my undergarments and clothes. I pull on my underwear, bra, and pants by the time Max appears behind me.

"Shera, why was my story so personal to you?" he repeats. "Tell me what happened."

I sigh as I turn to look at him. "Max, please give it a rest. I'm sorry I went off—it's late, we've been drinking, I'm tired—"

"Was it something with Elliot?"

Ice crawls up my spine, but I hold firm, sending whatever strength I have left toward the fortification of my mental walls.

"It's not important." I turn my attention to my personal belongings, still lying on the sofa. I've all but forgotten about my phone—my only connection to the real world. It glows, and when I pick it up, a waterfall of message previews from Lexi cascades down the screen. A text from 1:33 a.m. catches my eye: *Ugh, Emily came to the party and blacked out. She threw up a little on Scott Disick's shoe, and now she's crying about "getting old."* The current time, I note with a throb of anxiety, is 2:47 a.m.

"It is important," Max insists. "I can see it written all over your face."

"I don't owe you an explanation!" I exclaim, whirling on him. "We met a few hours ago. *This*"—I gesture wildly between us—"is not normal. We don't actually know each other, but we're standing here fighting like we've been together for years." A small smirk hides beneath his lips, raising the temperature of my already boiling blood. "Do you not see how fucking *strange* that is?"

"Well, I, for one, think it's better than normal." He shrugs, his demeanor shifting to the air of command and control I observed back at Bar Sperl. "There's been something very freeing about putting everything out there on the table all at once."

He's right. I've been more myself since our first interaction than I have been with most of my nearest and dearest in over a year. He also felt the full force of my anger, an emotion I always water down before serving it to any other man, ever. Somehow, I knew he could handle it—that he could hold it without being burned. Still, I can't give in—I can't risk uncorking myself. I can't risk giving him all of that when nothing beyond this night is promised.

I shake my head with a labored sigh, dragging my hands over my face. To both of our surprise, I let out a small, strained scream into my palms. When I peek through my fingers, Max appears to be stifling a laugh, but his brows knit together with a look of concern. He steps closer, closing the gap between us. I continue to cover my face.

"I won't ask anymore. You can tell me whenever you're ready or not at all," he assures me. "Now, what can I do to make you stay?"

I feel the warmth of his hands on my skin, fingers encircling my forearms, holding them firmly as if to tug my shield away. I shake my head again as he draws me to his chest, my body rigid at first, arms tucked in front of me as if to protect my heart. It *is* nice, I suppose—the ease between us, the comfortability. I wanted to leave before things got too heavy—as if that ship hasn't already sailed.

I surrender to his embrace. Our similar height allows me to lean my head perfectly against his shoulder, my nose grazing the crook of his neck. As I take a deep, cleansing exhale, his hands travel rhythmically over my back, soothing, as if I were a small child.

"I could eat something," I say, more of a declaration than a response to his question. The roiling, watery emotion in my belly has subsided, replaced by the gnaw of hunger. My pre-date anxiety meant I was only able to stomach a plate of crackers with cheese for dinner.

"Really?" A note of hope reverberates through his vocal cords. "I believe I can make that happen."

I pull away, sighing again as I look up at him. "What d'you got?"

Max can't help his triumphant smile as he leads the way, him shirtless and me in my bra. He flicks on a dangling Bauhaus pendant light as we enter the open dining room and kitchen and pushes aside the piles of notebook paper littering the table before he commands me to sit.

I slump wearily into one of the four cane dining chairs as I watch him open and close various cabinets, moving swiftly—presumably an effort to feed me before I remember my plan to leave.

"I'm not exactly set up for entertaining—it's been a while since anyone's been here, but"—he holds up a sleeve of capellini—"I can make pasta if that sounds alright?" His other hand holds a wilted bunch of parsley, a bulb of sprouted garlic, and a jar of sun-dried tomatoes.

"Sounds great—thank you," I reply. He nods and returns to the kitchen.

Max sets a pot of water to boil on the island cooktop and busies himself chopping the oily tomatoes and green-tipped garlic. I watch the ripple of his lean muscles with a pleasant flutter in my stomach, enjoying the feeling of quiet appreciation for his care. In a nonlinear way, we've crossed all the milestones of a typical relationship in a single night. The first kiss, then marriage, our first small argument, followed by some fooling around, then the first *big* fight, and now—our first dinner date. How it will end is still a mystery. At this rate, if I stay, there's a good chance we'll either buy a house together or file for divorce by morning.

"How do you feel about anchovies?" Max calls out, staring into a cupboard.

"Love them—when used sparingly."

"Noted," he replies, grabbing a small tin and carrying it to his workstation.

My mind goes pleasantly blank as I wait, turning my attention to the triptych of strangely ominous abstract art prints hanging on the wall beside me. I start to experience them as a colorful, midcentury modern Rorschach test, revealing the pain and panic I only just quelled, when Max announces that our food is ready.

"I'm really sorry, none of the proper dishes are clean at the moment." Max crosses to the table carrying a two-handled Le Creuset miniramekin and a Pyrex measuring cup, both filled with pasta. "Lady's choice?" He grins sheepishly as I laugh aloud for the first time in what feels like ages.

I squint, studying the two options. "I'll go with . . . the Pyrex." He hands me the piping-hot vessel along with an unopened packet of takeaway utensils. I watch as he settles into the seat next to mine with his own portion and smile to myself as I take my first bite.

"How is it then?" Max asks eagerly, twirling the thin noodles around his plastic fork as I chew thoughtfully.

"It's great, it's very—"

"*Jesus!*" Max exclaims, pushing away the ramekin and jumping up from his seat as if he's been bitten by something. He grimaces as he chews and swallows laboriously. "That's *disgusting!*"

I choke on the combination of laughter and capellini at his theatrical display as I force myself to swallow too.

"Oh, c'mon," I tease playfully, considering the steaming pasta. "So it's a little salty—"

"A *little*?" He inches forward as if even drawing near the small pot will put him at risk.

"How many anchovies did you use exactly?"

He drags a hand through his hair, mouth still agape. "Uh . . . only a couple, but—"

"Did you salt the water?"

Max claps a hand to his mouth as he nods silently.

"And did you add more to the pasta afterward without tasting it despite the anchovies *and* the tomatoes being *very* salty already?"

He drags his mouth slowly from his hands, his lips peeking just over his fingertips as he replies, "Yes—generously."

"Mystery solved." My shoulders shake with laughter as I smile pityingly at him before planting my fork back into the Pyrex. "The good news is, I happen to love salt—"

"I'm dead fucking serious, you can't eat that."

He steps toward me, reaching for my cup, but I grab it by the handle and hold it at arm's length away from him. Max cocks his head in response, raising his hands in surrender, but when I return the cup to the table, he lunges suddenly, this time successfully confiscating it from me.

"Sorry, but I'm making the call on this one," he says, backing away with the Pyrex in one hand and the ramekin in the other. "It'll have to be the emergency crisps."

"No!" I exclaim, watching with mock dismay as both containers go into the sink. As a preventative measure, Max turns on the faucet and floods our meal.

I can't control my laughter, and the warmth of it fills my body as Max opens the pantry and withdraws a large bag of salt and vinegar potato chips.

"Look, all evidence to the contrary—I *can* cook." He drops the bag on the table in front of me and takes a seat. "The pressure to impress had me rattled." He pauses, and I raise an eyebrow until he adds, "And I will never underestimate anchovies again."

"It's the thought that counts," I respond as I go for the bag.

We crunch comfortably without speaking for a few minutes. Despite his earlier promise, I can feel Max's thoughtful eyes still scanning, searching for answers as if they're written in the constellations of my freckles or hidden in the dark vines of my braids.

"Thanks for staying," he says abruptly, a look of genuine relief on his face.

I nod, drawing a knee to my chest as I lick the vinegary residue from my fingers. "I think the rules of this evening are the same as *Jumanji*. The die was cast, and now there'll probably be consequences if I try to leave before the game is finished—whatever that means."

"You know, I think you may be right—you might grow a tail if you go home."

Max rises, adjourning to the kitchen and returning with two glasses of water. My stomach flutters strangely at the gesture—as if the urge to hydrate is a harbinger of the night's impending end. Half an hour ago, I was lunging for the exit, but when he yawns suddenly, that small pang becomes the sound of a gong reverberating through me.

"Tired?" I ask sheepishly.

"Getting there," he says, tilting his head as he watches me. "But I don't have to be."

I feel him reading me, sensing my childlike desire to keep the next day from coming by simply refusing to succumb to the night.

"I could grab the bottle—"

"Yeah, why not?" I say a little too eagerly, eliciting a raised eyebrow. Max grins mischievously as he stands up from the table.

"Well, we've certainly had a few bumps in the road this evening, but overall, I'd say you're one hell of a good time, Shera—" He stops short. "I just realized I don't know your second name."

"Benoit."

"Shera Benoit," he muses, feeling it out for the first time. "Lovely to meet you."

I smile to myself as he leaves the room and returns with the vodka bottle in hand. I down the remaining water and offer my cup as he sits. No toast this time as we drink, wincing in unison at the burning liquid flooding our mouths. Fiddling with his phone, Max asks if I mind an encore of the "godfather of gloom." I agree, and the melancholic simplicity of "Chelsea Hotel #2" fills the room.

"You know, technically, you don't know my name either," he says, setting the phone aside. I give him a puzzled look. "My real name—" He pauses for dramatic effect and feigns a sigh. "Is Martin Doyle."

I blink, struggling to adjust to this oddly jarring news. "Martin" is an ill-fitting suit covering his slim, muscular frame, and "*Doyle*"—a pair of thick-rimmed glasses obscuring his chiseled face. So common in comparison to *Max King*, the effortlessly cool and quick-witted Casanova who sits before me.

"Oh my *god*—what other secrets have you been keeping from me?" My tone harkens back to our play-pretend marriage hours earlier. In the back of my mind, that stirring, intuitive voice that urged me to dig into his romantic past earlier shudders slightly at the thought of more hidden truths.

"I have a few," he says with a shrug. "I'll trade you for them—a secret for a secret." With that, he pours more vodka into both glasses, even though I've barely sipped mine. "It's a twist on the question game; they've got to be proper secrets—stuff you don't just share at the drop of a hat."

"Okay then, *Martin*," I reply with a smirk. "Ask away."

"Have you ever shoplifted?"

"Oh, c'mon," I snort. "No fluff. We're beyond that."

"Alright, alright, fine." He throws up his hands as he leans back. Several moments pass before he says, "Tell me a lie you've told that haunts you."

I see that honest, familiar curiosity in his gaze. Driven solely by a desire to know every part of me—the good, the bad, and the ugly. The answer swims into my mind immediately. Looking into Max's eyes, I suddenly want to unburden myself.

"Lexi and I were at a bar a few years back, and her ex-boyfriend Sam showed up. He was her first big love when she was twenty—totally broke her heart, and even though she always played it cool, I knew some small part of her was still hurt . . ."

The memory of their breakup lurches through my body. The call that woke me at 2 a.m. the night Sam ended things. Lexi never cried, even when we were kids—I'll never forget her guttural, aching sobs as she choked out the words over the phone, and I urged her to breathe while I dressed in seconds and found

111

my car keys. I stayed on the line with her the whole way to her apartment, only hanging up when I reached her doorway, and she collapsed into my arms. That night, I stroked her head until she fell asleep and resumed every time she woke—every time she cried out, remembering . . .

"I was alone, heading back from the bathroom, when Sam cornered me. I hated him for the pain he'd caused Lexi, but she always insisted that I be civil with him. Said it was a greater 'show of power' if we were friendly and unfazed—like he didn't even matter." I lick my lips. "That night I did my best, making small talk about bullshit, and he was friendly too, albeit a little drunk." I prop my elbow on the table and take a preparatory sip of my vodka before continuing. "Eventually, I said I needed to go find Lexi, and that's when he stopped me. Told me that he'd . . . always been in love with me. That Lexi had been a 'consolation prize,' and he couldn't hide it anymore."

The rage returns at the mere thought of it—those months following the breakup when I tended to my friend day and night, promising with everything inside me that he *had* loved her, that it *hadn't* all been a lie. I even allowed her a glimmer of hope when she begged me to tell her that there was always a chance they could get back together in the future, assuring her that when it comes to love, anything is possible. After Sam's confession, all of my consoling words became hollow.

"What did you say?"

"Nothing. I was in shock. I—I just bolted." I shake my head, processing the words I never repeated to a soul until now. "Turns out Lexi had been spying from across the room. She asked me if he'd said anything about her and"—a heavy sigh as I exhale my guilt—"I lied to her for the first time in our lives. Told her he'd said that losing her was the worst mistake of his life, but he knew he didn't deserve her."

Max huffs out a breath. "Sometimes the lies we tell to protect are the most poisonous ones."

I nod, going for another burning sip. I feel better somehow, but I don't want to dwell on it. I rack my brain for a question.

"Have you ever told someone you loved them when you didn't?"

I see the answer flash through his dark eyes before he says it. "Sean. I wanted to believe I could forget as well as forgive, but every time I've said it since . . . everything . . ." He trails off, and I nod, accepting the simplicity of his answer, annotating it with what he's shared already.

Max looks at me, eyes narrowing.

"Have you ever truly been in love?"

My lips part as I lunge for the obvious answer, but something stops me. "I—don't know," I admit, the words tumbling awkwardly from my mouth. "I thought so, but I've had to fight so hard for it in the past—sometimes I think maybe I've mistaken limerence for the real thing."

"I get that." He chuckles darkly as he sips his drink. I hesitate before my next question.

"What's your deepest regret?"

Max studies my face as a strange sadness comes into his eyes. "I know what you're hoping I'll say, but I can't be dishonest with you," he begins carefully. "It *was* the worst mistake of my life, one I'll never make again—but I wouldn't take it back." He looks at the ground from beneath his knitted brow. "I did burn my life to the ground that night, but I worked to rebuild, and I believe—I believe I've become a better man." His eyes lift to mine as his throat bobs. "I can't regret what happened, but—I'm afraid now that I've damaged something between us beyond repair with the weight of that mistake. As of tonight, I wonder if my deepest regret may be losing the trust of someone as wonderful as you."

I hold Max's gaze, my heart jumping at his words—straining against the protective barricades I tried to erect around it. I can practically smell the pile of secret truths and weighty lies smoldering between us. The intimacy of our earlier nudity meant nothing compared to this nakedness.

"I want to volunteer my next secret," I say, nearly a whisper. "It's the one you've been after."

XI

I close my eyes and take a deep, steadying breath. My mind works slowly, turning dead bolts, unknotting ropes, and cutting the razor wire encircling the memory. As the final padlock clicks open, I brace my hands against the table, feeling the wood grain beneath my fingers and reminding myself that I will not, in fact, be transported back in time through the portal of my memories. I look up to meet Max's gaze.

"There was this feeling of *fate* with Elliot from the start. We met at some art gallery opening downtown that neither of us had wanted to go to and ended up talking to each other all night." A sad half smile flickers across my lips. "He was an actor, and I'd never been crazy about actors, but he seemed different. Quiet and intelligent—sort of a thoughtful oddball in the best way." I rest my chin on my raised knee. "We were inseparable in the beginning."

For the first time in what feels like eons, I allow Elliot's face to materialize before me. His bright-blue eyes that crinkle at the corners when he smiles, his perfect teeth, his sloped nose and wavy hair. I see the two of us talking on the sofa. His hands on my face, fingers caressing my skin when he told me I was beautiful and our lips met for the very first time, soft and warm—like home.

I want to stop there, to hold nothing but the memory of how it started and let the rest fall away, but as I look at Max, as I remember what was already laid bare between us, I go on.

"Things started to change about two years in when Elliot was up for this supporting role in an A24 movie." My gaze becomes trancelike. "He made it through all the auditions, and we both really thought it was in the bag, but he lost it to someone else at the last minute." I bite my lip, furrowing my brow in concentration. "That experience, coming so close to what he wanted and losing it, triggered some kind of existential crisis." I continue as my tangled thoughts unravel one thin strand at a time. "I think it's something that happens when you grow up in LA—there's so much celebrity everywhere, you feel like being famous is the only option, and if you don't reach that goal by the time you're thirty, then you might as well be set adrift on the Pacific Ocean."

The image flashes into my mind. Elliot, sitting at the kitchen table with his head in his hands, hair mussed and falling around his face. I watched him, feeling his pain as my own and wanting to shine my light upon him, to cast out the darkness that had settled there and make him understand the beauty I saw when I looked at him. When I moved to stand behind him, wrapping my arms around his shoulders as my heart beat into his back, he stiffened, endured me for a few moments, then sat up and left the room.

"He stopped putting effort into his dreams. Instead, he surrounded himself with new people who put all their energy into drinking, partying, and rubbing elbows—he called it 'networking.'"

I let out a tired laugh. "He started avoiding me too, made secret plans I only found out about when friends told me they'd run into him at one bar or another." I pause, collecting my thoughts, the moments I tucked away and didn't dare to confront. "I told myself it was a phase."

Another searing vision. When he came home drunk and climbed into bed beside me as I lay turned away from him. When I felt his clumsy hands moving over my body and I told him I was tired. When he begged and pleaded against my firm declaration that I wanted him to stop. When at last I got up without a word to sleep on the couch, alone and confused as to why he rejected my willing advances for months but wanted it so desperately then—when I couldn't bring myself to give it.

"After a rough night, he'd apologize all morning, swearing he would change, but by every evening . . ." I down the last sip of my vodka with a grimace. "We started fighting daily. I told him he had to stop running and grow up, and he told me I didn't have a life, so I was obsessed with trying to control his."

Max lets out a sharp exhale, and the sound briefly brings me back into the room. His face is hardened.

"Honestly, he wasn't wrong," I admit, shaking my head with the realization. "I was so desperate for his love—the more he pulled away, the harder I held on. I *didn't* have a life. I was shrinking, becoming someone I didn't recognize—and the worst part was that I was doing it to myself . . ."

Another hazy memory creeps in. Sitting beside Elliot at a restaurant with all his cronies—sipping some drink I never wanted to begin with as he laughed and excitedly listened to the itinerary of the evening, the plan to hop from bar to bar, party to party, chasing glittering, empty promises and following endless Hollywood rabbit holes.

I didn't tell him—didn't even bother to mention that Lexi's family friend, a critically acclaimed novelist from New York gracious enough to read my manuscript, made time in her busy travel schedule to meet me for drinks that night. That she raved about my book and said she wanted to put me in touch with her literary agent—but I blew her off to join him for yet another aimless social outing. It was an act of self-sabotage, and I knew it—but it didn't matter. Not when I also knew that Elliot's dreams were dashed to pieces, and my potential success ran the risk of reminding him of that. Not when I felt that turning my attention elsewhere, to my own hopes and ambitions, posed the threat of driving us apart.

I put my hand on his knee under the table, desperate for the warmth of our connection—some sign that it was all worthwhile. He turned and smiled at me, beaming with that radiant light I hadn't felt in so long as his hand closed over mine. "I love you," he mouthed, and I whispered the same, just as a woman whose face I would never quite forget entered the restaurant and took her seat across from him at the table . . .

I turn my attention from the man inside my head to the one sitting before me. "I'll never really know what the catalyst was, but after nine months of what felt like endless turmoil, things started to change seemingly overnight." I shrug. "Elliot was suddenly optimistic and focused, avoiding his vices and the people that came along with them. He even suggested that we move to New York for a little—said he could really hone his craft without the celebrity culture creating a distraction, and I could find a better footing for my writing in a more 'intellectual setting.'" I shake my head. "I wanted to believe that we'd turned a corner, but I couldn't shake the feeling that something still wasn't right. In my gut, I just felt this sense of . . . foreboding."

My heart beats wildly as I clear my throat to continue, but before I can speak, Max reaches forward, his fingers grazing my hands as they move to grip my bent knee, hugged tightly against my body.

"You don't have to tell me, you know," he says, his face lined with concern. "You were right earlier—you don't owe me any explanation."

"I've had this story living inside of me for a year." My voice cracks as I push past the emotion. "I want to share it with you. I want you to understand why earlier I—"

"Alright," he says softly. "I understand. I'm listening." A beat of silence passes as we look at each other before Max gives a shallow nod, encouraging me to go on.

"It was February thirteenth—the night of my birthday. Something felt off from the start—we were at a bar with friends, and he was drinking heavily again," I continue, the script rolling out before me. "I asked him a few times what was wrong, but he insisted he was fine. I tried to let it go, but I really needed reassurance." My throat bobs as I shake my head again. "Eventually, I told him about the feeling I had—the intuition that something wasn't right between us." I look up as my vision blurs, blinking away the tears welling in my eyes. "He said if I fixated on the idea that something bad was going to happen, that I would create it."

I hear the words in Elliot's voice—see his once sparkling

blue eyes become steely with frustration, resentment, and fatigue. I remember my heart desperately fluttering, like a bird with a broken wing, as I swallowed my fears and nodded, putting on a brave face for my celebration.

"Around one, I wanted to go home—I was tired, and we were supposed to go to brunch with my mom the next day." I sniff as I surrender to my rising emotion, the first tear falling heavy and absorbing into the fabric of my pants. "I asked him to come home with me, but he was wasted, and his friends had just arrived."

The outer layers of my tale come away like corn husks. I can see the center now.

"I didn't want to give him the satisfaction of arguing, so I heaped on the passive aggression and told him it was fine. Said, 'I'll sleep at Lexi's. Go with the boys—I don't care.'" My voice breaks again at the sound of that line—the lie I told in hopes that he would see the pain in my eyes and make a different choice. "As we were saying goodbye, this girl walked over. I'd seen her before and had felt—an edge."

The restaurant scene—the night I bailed on the novelist—floods my mind again, and I see the face of that blonde seated across from Elliot. She watched the pair of us thoughtfully, asking questions and paying compliments. There was no hostility, no malice in her words or actions—but she made me nervous. Somehow, even then, I could *feel* her intentions.

I shift in my seat. "I was getting my purse when she grabbed Elliot's arm and told him it was time to go—like she was showing me she could take him away in an instant," I continue. "Before they left, the girl turned to me and said, 'Don't worry—I'll take good care of him.'"

My face is soaked now, tears flowing in a steady downpour, but before I have a chance to do so myself, Max reaches out and deftly wipes them away. When our eyes meet, I see the straining sorrow in his face—the yearning there to comfort me. I think of closing my fingers over his, of sinking deep into his touch, but I can't bring myself to do it—not now. The air around us tightens as his hand lingers against my cheek for a moment longer before he carefully draws it away.

"Who was she?" he asks.

"Someone who had the social currency Elliot wanted—some proximity to fame. At the end of the day—she didn't matter." I shrug defeatedly. "I compared myself to her for ages, trying to figure out why, but I realized she could have been anyone. She was the manifestation of my fears, and according to Elliot, I created her."

"You didn't 'manifest' that. That's a load of bollocks . . ."

"I was obsessed with the idea that he was ruining everything, slipping into bad habits, and falling in with the wrong people. Maybe I wanted to be right, to feel vindicated in some way and—and somehow I asked for it to happen—"

"You didn't ask for that, Shera," Max interrupts as he pulls his chair closer and uses his strength to turn mine toward him. He grips the chrome legs as his eyes bore into mine. "You didn't make it happen with your fucking mind. You saw that he was on a path of destruction—and yeah, maybe he put on a show for a little while, made it seem like he was back on the straight and narrow, but that voice inside was warning you."

It did warn me—that voice. I heard it when I went home with Lexi that night, as my stomach roiled with anxiety until I finally drifted off to sleep. I heard it when I awoke at 7 a.m. the next day and saw the blonde's face in my mind. I heard it, and I knew.

Another silence passes between Max and me for a moment before he asks bluntly, "So when did he tell you?"

It takes everything within me to breathe steadily—to keep the rasping, gasping mess of panic at bay. I ready the last piece to cast into the fire—to burn and release.

"He didn't," I say slowly, keeping time with the rhythm of my breath. "I left Lexi's early and headed home. Put my key in the door, stepped inside, and saw the bedroom door was closed." The blood roars in my ears as my heart pounds mercilessly, the scene unfolding before me with vivid clarity. "I turned the handle, opened it, and—" My voice quavers, but I force myself to say those final loathsome words.

"And there they were—together . . ."

Blonde hair fanned out over my pillow, his body curved toward hers—the peaceful, restful ease on both of their faces. The image that's been burned into my mind as if with a brand.

Looking at Max, at the horror on his face, I expect to break—but instead, my heart feels . . . *lighter*.

"What—" Max shakes his head, his words failing for a moment. "What did you do?"

"I screamed."

"What did *they* do?"

"They woke up," I say matter-of-factly. "I'll never forget when she saw me, she said, 'What the *fuck*?'—like I'd wandered in and fucked *her* boyfriend on *her* birthday."

A familiar feeling twists within my gut. In the aftermath, I saw the woman everywhere. Not literally, but in the face of anyone I met whose appearance or demeanor mirrored hers. My world turned to black and white—a binary in which I categorized every woman as either safe or unsafe. Ally or enemy. I did this with Emily; Michael's ex, Riley; and Sonia from the liquor store. I let my perception of all of them be colored by fear, by stories that didn't belong to them. They were not monsters, imperfect or otherwise. They were casualties of my hypervigilance—my need to remain on guard in a desperate attempt to keep that pain from ever finding me again.

I pause, allowing the realization of my misplaced judgment to work its way through me. I reimagine Sonia as an enthusiastic fan with enviable boldness. I see the rift between Emily and me with fresh clarity too. We're in a cocreated cold war, and at the end of the day, we both want the same thing: to love Lexi.

"Jesus, Mary, Joseph, and the donkey." Max breaks the silence, scrubbing his hands over his face.

I let out a soft laugh. "I spent the next two weeks in my childhood bed at my mom's house. Lexi never left my side . . ."

I smile, remembering how my tirelessly devoted best friend insisted on playing nurse, drawing baths, and brewing endless cups of tea. Once, she even tried to feed me in bed but ended up spilling warm butternut squash soup all over the both of us—the first time I was able to laugh after it happened.

"When I went back eventually, Elliot and I sat down and talked it all over." I look into Max's eyes, sad but steady. "By then, he'd become so detached—like his mind wouldn't allow him to access the guilt, so he just . . . intellectualized everything. Made it a 'shared responsibility.' We'd changed, grown apart. I'd driven him to it with all the pressure I created, and he'd been lost and weak—that was the story." I shook my head. "In the end, I asked if anything like that had ever happened before, and he just said, 'Well, not with *you* it hasn't.'"

I laugh suddenly, my eyes still glistening as the sound becomes louder and louder, and my shoulders begin to shake. Max watches me warily, surely wondering if this is the moment I crack up for good.

"I'm sure this isn't what you expected when you invited me back to your place." I laugh as I wipe away my fresh tears. "The worst part is the self-betrayal—I knew we weren't happy, *I* wasn't happy, but I put up with all of it because, maybe on some level, it's what I thought I deserved. I *chose* to abandon myself, my goals, my dreams—all in the name of holding on to him. With time, I know I can forgive Elliot—but I still don't know how to forgive myself."

The last of my truth, set to crackle, smolder, and burn to ash—I see the reflection of it there in Max's far-off eyes. The guilt, the pain—the recognition.

"*This*," I continue, gesturing toward the intricate, unseen webbing we constructed between us, "is the closest I've gotten to anything remotely romantic since it happened." I sniff noisily, abandoning any concern for my appearance. "My secret is I'm far from okay. For this whole fucking year, I've been like a traumatized dog from a shelter you have to retrain every single day so it learns not to be afraid of hats or umbrellas." I snort another laugh, my breath stuttering. "Now you know. I'm sorry—I know it's a lot."

He says nothing as I cry, my shoulders slumping with the

relief of release. I don't even move to shield my face, I realize—I feel none of that self-consciousness here, with Max, tonight.

Wordlessly, Max stands and pulls me to my feet, wrapping my body in his arms for the umpteenth time. I surrender to his comfort, breathing him in—a scent that has become so comforting, so familiar, so quickly.

"It is a lot," he says soothingly as he holds me, his hand cradling my head against him. "But you're not carrying it alone anymore."

XII

"Let's get some air," he says, giving me a tight hug.

I pull back from our embrace, looking up at Max through my bleary eyes. He cocks his head toward the window, to the deck encircling the stilted house.

"Trust, it'll feel good," he says with a wink. "I'll get you something warm to wear."

I miss the heat of his body immediately as I stand there like a hollowed-out fruit—scraped of my seeds and meat. Max returns wearing sweatpants, a black hoodie, and slides. In his arms, he carries a heavy wool coat, a scarf, and a pair of thick socks. I raise an eyebrow at the sight of our mismatched ensembles.

"Are we going . . . on an expedition?" I sniffle again.

"No, but given the way you've been shivering all night when it's probably twenty-two degrees in here—" He pauses at my puzzled face. "That's like seventy Fahrenheit."

"Oh. Yeah, I run cold."

"So, put these on."

Max helps me into the coat, buttoning me all the way up like a child heading off to school. I slip on the too-long socks, and he wraps the scarf around my head and neck like a makeshift hood.

We make our way to the living room and out through the glass sliding doors that open onto the deck. The chilly air is invigorating—I feel the coming transition from the darkness of night to the misty realization of morning as we look out over the reservoir. Through the trees below, the bright moonlight fans out over the black water, glistening and dancing to the intermittent orchestra of nocturnal animals.

"Want one?"

I turn to see Max offering me a cigarette, and I consider for a moment. "No—I'm good. I only smoke as a social crutch."

Max laughs as he lights his, the fire illuminating the chiseled line of his cheekbones as it had hours earlier—in another lifetime.

"You want to know something funny?" he says as he exhales. "I don't even smoke."

"What?"

He pinches the bridge of his nose, wincing as if he's said too much but now has no choice but to reveal himself.

"Back at the bar, we were standing there, and I felt like you were warming up to me, but I wanted a reason to get you on your own." He shrugs, an easy, honest smile overtaking his face. "Asking you to join me on a quest for cigs seemed natural enough—but I actually quit seven months back."

"I guess I should be flattered that you did all that just to lure me in," I snort as a shiver runs through me despite Max's preemptive bundling.

I feel a small current of electricity between us as he moves toward me. I long for him to pull me close against the cold but say nothing. I hesitate for a moment before telling him, "Thank you, by the way—for listening, I mean."

He meets my gaze and nods, the smoke intermingling with his breath and swirling up into the air before us. "You know, I see a lot of myself in Elliot—as much as I don't want to." He leans forward, his forearms resting over the railing as he looks out on the sleepy streets below. "Being seduced by all the shiny bullshit, wanting to be 'someone' and to escape the pain so badly that you end up taking the real ones for granted." He shakes his head. "But on the other hand, I see myself in you—feeling so desperate to hold on that you lose yourself along the way. Doing what I did, staying with Lilah until I snapped and—" He pauses, hesitating before continuing with firm assurance. "Cheated—that was self-betrayal too. It went against everything I knew about myself. Against everything I swore I would never become . . ."

As he trails off, I sense that he's holding both of his parents in mind—Saint Catríona the Patient and his father, whose torment and betrayal she weathered for decades.

"I understand," I murmur. "It's . . . complicated."

A colossal understatement, but my mind feels stretched and thin. I lean against the railing and look up, drawing in the crisp air as I take in the beaming moon in its entirety for the first time.

"I forgot it's a full moon," I muse, almost to myself. "Maybe that explains it—it really has been quite a night."

Max nods, following my gaze upward. "And to think, I almost missed it."

"What do you mean?"

He's silent for a moment—I feel him searching for an entry point, something he wants to say.

"What is it?" I urge with a hint of apprehension.

"I wasn't at Bar Sperl just having a drink by myself," he says. "I was trying to work up the nerve to meet someone—a girl."

My veins turn icy at the words, but I breathe steadily. "A girl? Someone you're . . . seeing?"

"No, no," he assures me, sensing my uneasiness. "Just someone I was meant to meet up with—temporarily."

"Are you saying you stood up a booty call and invited me home with you instead?"

"Not exactly."

I match his steady gaze as he takes a final drag, the embers glowing bright orange as the burning tobacco crackles in the silence. I watch him anxiously as he tamps out the smoldering butt against the bottom of his shoe and sets it on a waiting table before returning to his post beside me.

"I was half set on meeting this girl, but—I wanted a clear sign if it was the right move. If it was the right decision." I raise an eyebrow as he resumes. "I was sitting there drinking and mulling it over when I looked up and saw you." The moonlight illuminates the small smile that comes to his lips. "And I suppose once we spoke, it felt like divine providence. A sign that I wasn't meant to follow through on my previous plans."

I ignore his poetic flattery, looking out toward the water. "Why was it such a difficult decision to make—with the girl, I mean?"

He sighs as he turns toward me with a look I now know well: the tired acceptance that somehow, by whatever magic has woven between us, we're powerless to conceal the truth from each other.

"I've had a few . . . flings since Lilah, but nothing serious. When I decided to sort my life out, focus on my art, and start fresh, I went on a bit of a cleanse." He holds my gaze steadily as he says, "No more meaningless sex."

"Really?" I can't help my tone of surprise.

He laughs and licks his lips as he leans in toward me. "Is that so hard to believe?"

"No, I mean, it's just—" I falter, flashing again to Sonia's bold admiration at the liquor store—a regular occurrence, I imagine. "I'm just impressed—with your restraint."

Max's eyes dance with mirthful light as he watches me. "Well, anyway—I've kept to that rule and haven't been with anyone in a good while now, but yesterday, just casually scrolling through Instagram, I discovered that, um—" He pauses, looking down as his fingers trace the wood grain of the railing. "That Lilah's engaged again."

My eyes snap to his. "Not to—"

"Jesus, no," Max interrupts before I even have a chance to utter his bassist's name. "To some billionaire—a French one." He snorts haughtily. "Shouldn't have got to me, but it did. Maybe because I know if she was here, she'd be saying, 'Look at me now—I've won.'"

"There is no winning," I say quietly.

"True," he replies with a small sigh. "But it still got to me—my ego, I suppose." His eyes are far off and contemplative as they search the darkness ahead, but they're not pained as they were before. "Earlier, when I was being a prick about you going for Michael, and you said you felt like you *needed* to fuck him—well, I may have understood that more than I let on." He shrugs. "After hearing about Lilah, I decided I needed to fill the void with a good old-fashioned empty fuck." I watch the side of his face as he chuckles ruefully, concealing what appears to be a genuine sense of shame. "So I texted a girl I'd already had a go with before, and it turned out she was up for a repeat performance."

"So you saw me and decided . . . what exactly?" I ask after a long moment.

Max turns and gently pulls back the scarf encircling my head and neck. "As I've said," he begins slowly, eyes roving over me as if his answer is written across my face, "I was completely taken with you. Your eyes, your lips, the way you moved—your essence." My heart flutters as he bites his lip, shaking his head while he watches me. "But then we spoke, and you were—*deadly* sharp. Like a blade cutting through all my charms, hacking my game to bits." He laughs. "I wanted to know you, and I didn't care if anything came of it. I didn't need a conquest." I swallow hard as he draws nearer still. "And I knew that if by some miracle we did fuck, there wouldn't be anything meaningless or empty about it."

I wonder if Max can see my cheeks in the moonlight, flushing with color at his words. My entire body pulses with my heartbeat, thundering so loudly, I'm almost certain he can hear it too. His face is so close, I can smell the whisper of smoke on him as his lips part invitingly and his hands move to my waist.

I want nothing more than to give myself over to those hands, that mouth. To surrender to his entire being and melt into his touch, but I feel the night air changing—foretelling of dawn. Of the next day and the question of what's to follow. I want to let go, to free my heart and accept the risk—but even as I look into his eyes, I can feel something fearful within me resist.

"Can we go in?" I ask abruptly, a violent shiver tearing through me. "I'm losing feeling in my limbs."

Max raises his eyebrows dramatically, observing the tremor of my chattering teeth. "So *delicate*." He tsks, brushing a thumb over my cold cheek, the pad warm and soft against my skin. "Alright then, before you lose a toe."

Back inside, we silently agree to return to the bedroom with an unspoken understanding that I won't try to escape again. After I put on my borrowed Thin Lizzy tee and boxer briefs again, Max offers me a fresh toothbrush and remarks that I have free rein of whatever I need from the medicine cabinet.

I ready myself for sleep in the bathroom, enjoying the soothing ritual as I wash away the dried tear streaks and flaking mascara that have presumably marred my face for hours. After I brush my teeth, clean my face, and make good use of Max's surprising assortment of high-end skin products, I return to the bedroom.

The duvet still bears the impressions of our earlier activities as I climb under the soft linen covers for the first time. Max enters then, carrying a steaming earthenware mug.

"Chamomile tea for the hypothermia patient?"

I nod with a smile and accept the cup as I watch him undress again, stripping down to his underwear. When he catches my gaze wandering involuntarily over his chest and muscled legs, he raises his eyebrows. I roll my eyes in response and busy myself with blowing on the piping-hot liquid before taking a careful sip.

"You know, I can feel that you're still a bit wary of me," Max says as he climbs in beside me.

"I hope you know that it's not about judgment," I reply as I set my mug aside. "It caught me off guard when you told me about what happened with Lilah, in part because up until that point, I'd been enjoying my time with you almost like a vacation from all the mess of my own past. Sex, drinking, honesty, freedom—all the things that were dark and *tainted* in my life suddenly felt safe and fun in this no-strings fantasy world." I sigh as I look toward the ceiling. "But then two things happened: One, I started to see the truth of who you are, the person beneath the mask, and I felt like I could—" I swallow hard against the constriction of my throat as I force myself to say the words aloud. "Could potentially care very deeply about that person—in the real world."

"And the other thing?" Max is still as stone, but I sense the swirling mass of complex thoughts and emotions behind his dark eyes.

"I was confronted with my deepest fear—that it's not as simple as choosing good people over bad people, heroes over villains. Everyone is capable of betrayal—it's human nature to act selfishly," I answer. "There are no safe bets—no matter what, if I get close to someone, I'll always run the risk of it happening again."

"Within those two realizations, I see two philosophies of life itself." Max turns onto his side to face me. "The latter is fairly grim—that people are inherently untrustworthy and all love is just the appetizer to an inevitable feast of pain." He shakes his head. "That's no way to live, especially when to do so, you'd have to ignore the deep, true love you experience every single day."

I think of Lexi. Our unwavering loyalty to each other—the force of that unbreakable bond. A sisterhood upheld not by blood, not by obligation, but by our commitment, trust, and love for each other.

Max licks his lips, a half smile nestling in the corner of his mouth. "As for your first realization, what I gather is that being

here, getting to know me—you started to feel a sense of hope."
My eyes flick to his, and he holds my gaze as he says, "Wasn't it
Emily Dickinson who said, 'Hope is the thing with feathers—it
perches in the soul and sings and never stops at all'? Or something like that—I don't remember exactly." I smile as he runs a
hand over his face. "The point is that hope will always persist.
It doesn't need to be rationalized or analyzed, and it would be a
cruel, foolish thing to try to silence it when you hear its song."

"That was beautiful," I say gently. "Have you considered
songwriting—?"

Max reaches over, squeezing my exposed side in answer to
my mischievous, mocking tone. I squirm away instinctively, but
he uses the moment to draw me closer. I know that despite my
deflection, he can feel my acceptance of his words—the sage
truth of them.

"No one can predict how anything will turn out. Outside
of this house—in the 'real world,' as you put it—it could be a
nightmare. Like those characters in your novel, we could find
that we've both fallen for a fantasy of each other." His hand
rests on the curve of my side, thumb gently caressing. "But I
have a feeling that's not the case. Not when I already know you're
a traumatized shelter dog with sleep issues who's prone to panic
attacks." I laugh, burying my face in my hands. "And you know
I'm a reformed adulterer and opportunistic smoker with mammy
and daddy issues—"

"Who can't cook," I add from behind my palms.

"Who *can* cook," he corrects as he tugs my hands away,
and I let him. Our eyes meet as he reclines, gripping my wrists,

and something tightens between us like the tension of a drawn bowstring.

"Who would like another shot at redemption," he continues, his gaze flickering to my mouth. "In more ways than one."

Out of order, out of sequence. We crossed into the territory of physical intimacy hours ago, and yet . . . my nerves feel fresh, brand new. Not because I'm afraid of approaching a threshold we have yet to cross. But because my feelings have changed. Deepened, somehow, in just a few short hours.

More at stake. More to lose.

I think of them again—my two flawed characters who leave the dream and find each other in the real world. I still don't know how the story ends—if they destroy each other and fall into ruin or choose love, fighting through the darkness. One thing I do know is that by whatever power, whatever strange enchantment has been woven over the evening—I can feel them *stirring* again within me. The piston finally pushing at the crankshaft of my long-rusted creative engine, rumbling with a renewed desire to write again. To finish the story.

More at stake. More to gain.

I track Max's eyes for a moment before my gaze falls to his lips. It would be so simple, so easy to lean in toward that mouth. To risk my complete and utter undoing for a chance at those endless possibilities.

XIII

As if sensing the mess of thoughts tangled in my mind, Max releases my hands. An easy smile spreads over his face as he settles back in, reclining on his side in his subtle way of showing me once again that there's no pressure.

"Your tea's probably going cold," he says with a jerk of his nose toward my bedside.

"You know, I have a theory that no one really drinks tea."

Max flashes a look of amusement. "Try telling that to the whole of the UK—"

"Tea is universally symbolic of comfort, correct?" I ask, ignoring his commentary. He nods with a laugh as I go on. "But it's not about *drinking* it. Boiling the water, pouring it, letting it steep—that's the ritual, that's the good part."

"You didn't even get to do the boiling and brewing yourself," he says with mock dismay. "I *robbed* you of that comfort."

"True," I reply with the fervor of a mad scientist in the midst of cracking a complex formula. "But tea can also be used as a symbol of care—a gesture toward someone else. The comfort comes then when you receive the cup, when you understand that the tea *giver* cares for you and wants to put you at ease, but the beverage itself"—I gesture dismissively toward the nightstand—"is useless."

Max watches me, eyes twinkling. "I love the way you make mundane things feel fantastical. You say everything with such conviction and confidence, even when you're having a laugh—a true storyteller."

"Thanks." A small flame of pride ignites within me. "I have to admit, I haven't been this way in a long time, but—I feel like I caught glimpses of my old self tonight." I smile, recognizing my feelings as I articulate them. "I used to be much bolder, more self-assured, '*sharp* and *cutting*'—like you described." A flicker of sadness passes through me. "That last day when Elliot was divvying up our faults, he said he missed that girl, that he didn't like who I'd become—but I think I knew that if she came back, I would've had to leave. There's no way *she* would've put up with his shit." I try to laugh it off, but Max turns to me, his expression grave.

"He was just pulling you apart to prop himself up."

"Maybe he was," I reply. "But there was some truth to it—I had changed." I blow out an exhale as I look into his eyes. "I really have done my best to clean my side of the street. I just wish he could've dealt with his. Instead, I've had to accept the picture of what happened, feeling incomplete, like a puzzle that's missing all the corner pieces."

Max studies me, his eyes flashing over my features, reading and scanning. There's no use in hiding—I accept the way he probes around gently.

"Pretend I'm him."

"What?"

"I'm Elliot," he says with a shallow nod. "Ask me anything."

"Improv again?" I let out a breathy laugh, but Max's expectant stare is unflinching.

"Okay." I draw in breath and release a weighty exhale as I lie on my side to face him. "Elliot, tell me why you really did it."

"I wasn't happy with myself—with my life," Max begins. "I couldn't deal with reality, so I decided to fill the void with fleeting pleasure and surface achievements. Deep down, I felt like I didn't deserve your love, so I pushed you away—but the more you held on, the harder it became to face the truth." My breathing quickens as he holds my gaze. "I couldn't bear the weight of failing you anymore, so I decided to destroy my life—to blow it all to bits once and for all, because—" He shakes his head, some true feeling of disbelief and regret welling within him. "You loved me so much, I knew it was the only way you'd walk away."

We stare at each other as those words settle over us. I imagine his warm brown eyes turning pale blue; his sharp, prominent nose becoming smaller and more rounded; the delicate bow of his lips firming into a broad, hard line. Like night and day, dusk and dawn.

"I'm sorry, Shera," Max continues with feeling, still in character. "I'm sorry I didn't cherish and protect you the way you deserved, I'm sorry my demons became your nightmares, I'm sorry my indifference made you feel undesirable, and I'm sorry my actions made you doubt how easy it is for someone to love you."

A strange relief washes over me in the silence, and my quivering lips form a small smile as a silent tear rolls down my cheek.

"Thank you," I whisper. Max nods, wiping a tear as it travels over my cheekbone.

"Okay." I sniff, sitting upright as I turn to face him. "Your turn." Max lifts a curious eyebrow but shifts himself higher on his elbows as I close my eyes. With my exhale, I open them.

"I'm Lilah now." Max chuckles softly as he opens his mouth to speak, but I interrupt. "I've already heard your apologies, and I think we both know that you've paid for what you did to me." He watches me curiously as I sink into the consciousness of his ex-fiancée. "At the end of the day, your choices were your own—but I want to tell you that I'm sorry too. I contributed to creating a familiar environment that eventually led you to act out in . . . familiar ways." He nods, his hand moving instinctively to the tattoo above his heart. "I believe in redemption—I see that you've worked hard to become a better man, and you are not your lowest moments." I swallow hard. "I forgive you, Max."

His eyes jump to mine, blinking rapidly as he processes all that I said as Lilah—and as myself.

"Thank you, Shera." His breathing is measured as he reaches up, laying his palm to rest against my cheek, his thumb caressing the skin at the corner of my mouth. "For everything."

A choice presents itself again in the warmth of his touch—the way it pours through me like molten silver. I can pull away, and he'll let me without protest, those embers in his eyes dwindling until we eventually find our way to sleep. Later on, I'll carry the events of the night in my back pocket, and eventually, it will become a distant memory of a long, strange encounter and nothing more.

Or I can take a flying leap. I can heed Max's wise words and stop trying to silence the song of hope.

I turn, almost imperceptibly, toward the warmth of his hand until his thumb brushes against my lower lip. His eyes follow, trailing to my mouth, and he pauses, his bare chest heaving slightly. I steady myself as he looks up to meet my eyes, a question thinly veiled behind his unwavering stare. In answer, I part my lips, pressing them against the pad of his thumb as he did hours earlier in the wake of our first kiss, meeting the force of his gaze with equal might.

With that silent agreement, his soft demeanor firms. He drags his touch over the flesh of my lips, back and forth. I watch as his muscles draw taut, his breath rising and falling in time with my own, and I know that any worry or hesitation will have to wait until morning.

I break from his touch and pull off my shirt, feeling his eyes on my breasts, on the points of my rosy-brown nipples as my bare skin meets the air. Lying back against the pillows, I pull him to me, hungry for the kiss I've denied the both of us for hours on end. He holds my face in his hands as our lips crush together in a perfect fit, soft and warm. With every fluid, cursive movement of our mouths, I draw him deeper, wrapping my arms around his chiseled form, locking him against me.

He moves from my mouth, trailing an achingly slow procession of kisses down my neck and along my breasts. I can feel his smile in the broad expanse of his lips, his breath hot against me as I writhe beneath him.

"Please," I whimper as the wetness of his lips leaves stinging patches of cold air along my searing skin. "I *need* you to fuck me."

Max stops suddenly, rising up to meet my gaze. I stare back, my face fixed in a pained, breathless expression. "I know that's what we both want," he says. "But I don't want to hear it until you really mean it, do you understand?"

I blink. His eyes are filled with the same honesty I've seen all night. Something in the sincerity of his tone is arresting. No game, no bravado as he searches my face once again for the truth.

My yearning is genuine, but the unconsciously copy-and-pasted performance—the pleading, begging, and needful way I'd learned that men like it—was from a generic, practiced playbook. With all the buildup and tension, I wanted to put on a show, to be whatever I thought he wanted me to be, but as with every other pivotal moment we had, he just wants me to be truthful.

"Okay," I murmur. "I understand."

"Good." His voice deepens as his fingers dive beneath my waistband, plunging into me in one fluid motion. I gasp, an involuntary release as he sinks in deeper, feeling the truth of my desire, wet and wanting but not yet at the point of need that he requires before I can say those words.

I close my eyes as he moves his hand, slowly at first, studying the pattern of my breath. I don't force any sound. His unoccupied hand holds my face, and his lips return to mine, enveloping my sharpening exhales with his kiss as the rhythmic beckoning of his fingers quickens.

Max pulls away and sits back on his heels, gripping my bent knees, and my eyes shoot open with the sensation of sudden vacancy. I prop myself up on my elbows, watching his eyes meander from mine, down my sternum, and further still as he carefully slides off my underwear. He regards me with awe, and already, it's a familiar sight.

When he rises up on his knees, framed perfectly by my own, and tugs off his underwear, my heart jumps wildly observing the state of him. Impressively, *staggeringly* hard—without question.

A cocky half smile spreads across Max's lips as he pushes my legs farther apart and settles in between them, diving forward as our lips resume. I can't help my hips grinding up to meet his as I feel the bare warmth and length of him, so dangerously close, but his hand goes to my rising hip, restraining, holding firm. I feel the change, instinct overriding intellect. My blood turns fiery again at the feeling of his control, and as if he senses it, his fingers dig deeper into my flesh, fighting the muscled undulation of my body. His hand encircles my throat, gripping the sides as his own sounds of restraint reverberate through me.

I'm burning, aching now—fully and completely. My movements beneath him become intentional, desperate attempts to pull him inward, to feel him at long last. I fight for alignment, but he bests me, refusing over and over again, lifting his hips as if in punishment for my impatience. That was his mistake. I thrust upward, and he sinks into me for just a moment, a mutual groan escaping both our lips before he pulls away entirely.

Max pants, smiling wickedly at the cat and mouse of it all as he watches my heaving chest. Wordlessly, he leans over, withdrawing a condom from its hiding place within the nightstand drawer as I wonder briefly when exactly during the evening he snuck away to stash them. He holds my gaze for a moment as he tears the wrapper with his teeth and spits the remnants aside before rolling it over himself.

The weight of him returns, heavy and firm against my center, and I grip his sides with my knees like the body of a cello. I lean forward to taste his lips again, but he pulls back, holding my face steady as if attempting to memorize every feature with his touch, capturing every breath, every sigh, every sound. His hand slips downward, and I feel him then, positioning—poised and ready. I don't move as his eyes bore into mine, admiring or maybe searching before he eases forward at long last.

I suck in breath at the sensation. It's been a very long time, but even still—he's barely in, and it's an effort to urge myself to relax. Another inch forward, and the feeling of fullness is so overwhelming, I can hardly imagine more. Finally, he kisses me—deeper and more fervent now as my body begins to open, melting around him. I wind my hands into his hair, demanding his lips and tongue, and he carefully drives the whole of himself into me, deeper and deeper. I moan into his mouth, waiting for more and bracing for the movement of his hips, but instead, without warning—he withdraws.

Emptiness. Horrible, *sickening* emptiness as he pulls away from my ravenous kiss, leaving me cold and hollow, save for the burning, agonizing heat between my legs.

"*Max.*" His name tumbles from my mouth before I have a chance to stop it.

His familiar, devilish smile returns as he leans in, his arms a rippling, muscled cage around my shoulders. As I burn and heave beneath him, he asks, low and slow beside my ear, "Yes, Shera?"

"I need you to fuck me."

The air leaves my lungs as he plunges every inch into me, hard and swift. I cry out, but his mouth muffles the sound, feeding, devouring as I buck my hips against the rolling tide of his every thrust. The room, the house, the world around us vanish as we draw closer than flesh, time swirling and bending with every jumping inhale and exultant exhale. Every stretching, filling, warming drive of his body tears the sound from my throat—the undeniable truth of my complete and utter surrender.

There's no telling if seconds or years have passed when I feel the building pressure deep within, like the gathering of a colossal wave as my breath leaps higher and higher. Sensing my undoing, Max forces my arms above my head, encircling both wrists with a single broad hand while the other grips my chin.

"Look at me," he orders, his voice rasping and earnest when I meet his gaze. His unrelenting, yearning brown eyes drive deeper into me than anything else.

I can't hold on any longer. I fight to maintain his unabating stare through a final tremendous thrust before fire erupts, covering me in shimmering darkness as my body shakes and heaves against him, surge after surge shuddering through my entire being. I feel Max's climax follow moments after, his lips finding mine as he groans and breathes through spasms of tension and release until we both fall still.

Blinking open my eyes, I realize I dozed off, and I don't know for how long. I roll on my side and see the undrunk tea sitting just beside me on the nightstand. I become aware of the hands encircling my waist. The body curling along my spine, encasing me in warmth as I listen to the easy ebb and flow of breath in my ear. I'm careful as I slip from Max's embrace, lifting his arms tenderly as I slide to the edge of the bed.

"And where do you think you're going?"

I start at the sound of his voice, breathing a laugh as I turn to look at him. "I was just going to turn off the light," I reply, smiling at the sight of him.

"Fair enough."

He stretches as I walk to the paper lantern and extinguish its golden glow. As I shuffle back to the bed, my eyes flick to the alarm clock, and a jolt of surprise runs through me when I see the digits "5:42 a.m." beaming brightly.

"It's so *late*—or early." I stage whisper, crawling under the sheets beside Max as he absorbs me back into his arms.

"*Shh.*" He sleepily presses a finger to my lips from behind. "Here's what's going to happen: we're going to sleep until we feel like getting up, and then we'll go out for breakfast," he murmurs, hugging me tighter as he breathes into the crook of my neck.

Max's arms grow heavy while I watch the faint blue of new dawn creep around the edges of the curtains, roving over the ground to wake the rest of the world from its slumber as we drift into ours. The untouched darkness still holds all we shared, and I feel the presence of those old ghosts there too. Echoes of our former lives, the reasons and reckonings for who we are and where we come from—the cautionary tales we watch closely in the rearview mirror.

Soon, my own eyes flutter and laze, and I watch those specters leave at last—fading with the light as I listen to the birds outside sing their trilling songs for a new day.

You don't have to leave Shera and Max after one night. Immerse yourself in their world with a taste of what happens after they awake, their musical influences, and the objects that shape their story. There may even be a Nicole and Warren moment waiting for you. Scan here or visit 831stories.com/hardlystrangers.

ACKNOWLEDGMENTS

I want to take a moment to express my gratitude to all those who helped bring this book into being. It was a meandering, often emotional journey, and I'm so thankful for everyone who helped me work out the kinks and knots both on and off the page, guiding me through to the very last keystroke.

First and foremost, to my publishers, Claire Mazur and Erica Cerulo: I remember being struck with a feeling of fate when I received your email as I sat looking out over the coastline at the Esalen Institute in Big Sur. I was there on a soul-searching mission and had only just spoken aloud to those sea cliffs and asked for a sign that I was meant to be a writer. At the time, despite the synchronicity, I let practicality override faith and assumed it was too good to be true, but luckily, you were both persistent. Thank you, both of you, for taking a chance on me and for your boundless encouragement and trust throughout.

As a first-time author, the editing process was a terrifying concept, but Michelle Flythe and Sanjana Basker immediately put any fears I had to rest. Every unique insight was like a gentle offering—I felt assured in culling what didn't serve the story and safe in protecting the soft, tender parts. I deeply appreciate you both for just "getting" it and handling this work with care.

To Katrina Leno: For years, every time I melted into a puddle of uncertainty about my life, you used that interminably dry, comedic tone of yours and told me, in so many words, to "stop crying and start writing." When this opportunity arose, it was your voice that provided the most reassurance. Thank you for telling me I could do it and for always bullying me into a sense of confidence.

Maman and Papa, you already know. Thank you for pushing me to take the road less traveled and for always assuring me in the special way that only parents can that this is indeed my path.

Frank, it's been said that a broken heart can only be mended in solitude, and while I believe that I could've healed without you, I'm glad I didn't have to. Thank you for pushing me to do this; for weathering every chaotic, tumultuous moment of my writing process; for feeding and watering me; and for having the patience to teach me every day that I need not be afraid of hats or umbrellas anymore.

I would be remiss if I didn't share my gratitude for you too, Leo. Even when it hurt, you always told me I could do anything I set my mind to. Life has a funny way of working out—if it weren't for you, this would be a very different story. I'll tell you the other version sometime—maybe in another life when we're both cats.

Last but certainly not least, to the man behind Max King: My time with you, however brief, will always be remembered fondly. I don't know if you'll ever read this, but I thank you for a good time and an even better story.

ABOUT THE AUTHOR

ALANA CLOUD-ROBINSON, who writes under the name A.C. Robinson, is a poet, essayist, and novelist from Los Angeles, California. She was raised on English Romanticism, Greek mythology, Beat poetry, and the slapstick comedic stylings of the Three Stooges. In 2022, she published *The Artists Are Frightened*, her premier collection of personal poetry.